# The Secrets He Kept

## A Novel by:

### Platinum

### &

### Sakeena Raheem

# Copyright Notice

# Chapter 1

"Winter, get up and let's go," Nancy whispered.

Winter sleepily stirred in the bed not knowing what was going on. Her heavy eyes started to close involuntarily, as she wiped them and tried to focus on her mother who was stuffing her clothes into a bag.

"What are you doing just sitting there, let's go!" Nancy said just above a whisper trying not to wake a sleeping Charles.

Winter could see the fear in her mother's eyes and hopped out of bed. "Mommy what's wrong? Where is daddy?" Winter whined.

"We have to go now." Nancy yanked Winter up by the arm.

Nancy drug Winter down the basement stairs and proceeded straight to the life size picture of her and Charles. She couldn't help but stare at how in love they both looked. The picture was taken back when Winter was a baby. She thought for sure he was ready to leave his wife for her but that day never came.

Nancy removed the picture, tossing it to the side. She put the code in with precision. Looking at all the money made her mouth water. She never saw that much money in her life. Charles had asked her can he put the safe in the house, but she never knew he was holding that much money. She would see him on a daily basis going downstairs with a duffle bag. Sometimes the bag would be empty and sometimes it would be full. She never questioned him about it.

Nancy had watched Charles and searched for the combination to the safe for weeks on end. One day, Charles left his phone laying on the nightstand while he was in the shower and she went through it. Finding a set of numbers in his phone, Nancy sent them to her phone via text message. She erased all evidence of her being in his phone and put it back where she had found it.

While Winter was at school one day and Charles was out on a run, Nancy took the numbers and tried every way possible to put the numbers in the safe combination and finally she got it open. She could see it held a couple thousands of dollars, some papers, bank statements and a gun. She closed and locked the safe, making sure she left it as it were.

Nancy begin removing all the money and stuffing it in Winter's backpack from school. Charles had to have been in the safe because the money that was there was not there a couple of days before. She grabbed the gun as well for safety. Before she walked away, she made sure she left the safe door open. Once Charles realized she was gone and as well as his money, she was sure he would come for her.

Nancy turned on her heels and threw the bag over her shoulder. She picked Winter up and put her on her hip. She didn't have time to explain to her six year old that if they didn't leave now, they both would be killed because of something she had done.

Nancy hit the ground running and never looked back. She picked up and left in the middle of the night with three bags. Two was she and Winter's clothes, and the other bag held five hundred stacks she stole from Winter's father.

"Ma!" Winter yelled again.

Nancy was brought back to reality by the sound of her daughter's voice. "Yes baby."

"You going to walk me to school?" Winter asked.

"Um, yeah Winter, let me grab my purse," Nancy answered.

Nancy walked into her room to get her purse. She had been thinking about that night she left Charles and had been scared lately. It had been almost five years since that day and nothing had happened. No sighting of Charles, no threats, and no harm has been caused. This was all strange to her. It was out of character for Charles not to come looking for her.

Nancy said a silent prayer to God before she walked out of her room to join her daughter. She grabbed ahold of Winter's hand and led her out the door. "When you get out of school, make sure you come straight home."

"Awe ma, why can't I go to Abe's house?" Winter pouted.

"Because I said so. I got to make a run later and want you in the house safely," Nancy sternly spoke.

Winter knew better than to talk back. "Yes ma'am," was all she could say. She was heartbroken to know she couldn't go to her friend's house. "Can we at least stop by his house so he can walk with us to school?"

"Why his mother or brother can't walk him to school?" Nancy asked.

Nancy didn't like the fact that Winter and Abraham were so close. They had been friends for four years. The bond the two had was one you only find in older people.

"Ma, his brother isn't home and his momma has been gone for days. He's home by his self," Winter stated.

"By his self?" Nancy mimicked.

"Oops," Winter responded, covering her mouth.

"Un uh, open your mouth and talk young lady," Nancy scolded.

"Ma, I promised I wouldn't say anything," Winter whined.

"How do you know that?" Nancy came back.

# The Secrets He Kept

"Because I talked to him this morning," Winter explained.

Nancy just looked down at her daughter and wondered how it was that she could be so strong-willed about a boy at such a young age. They stopped and picked up Abraham and continued their walk to the school. Nancy watched as the two kids interacted with each other.

Nancy made sure the kids got to school safely before making the two-block walk back home. Once Nancy made it home, she did her everyday routine and started cleaning the house. It was only Winter and her living there, so it wasn't much to clean. They had moved to the heart of Baltimore from Texas. She tried to put as much distance as she could between her old life and her new one.

The life she lived in Texas was one she didn't miss. Nancy was Charles side chick for ten years. Charles had promised that after Winter was born he would leave his wife, but he didn't. This hurt Nancy to her heart to know that she would never be his number one. She was tired of being walked all over and his well-kept secret. This is what prompted her to come up with the plan. She wanted to hurt Charles just as much as he hurt her. Nancy had been hitting Charles' pockets for weeks. She couldn't seem to get enough money so she devised with the plan of hitting the safe.

Nancy was bitter about the life she had lived for so long. Being stupid for Charles had sheltered her from the chances of being loved by someone who would have loved her whole heartedly. A couple days before she planned to leave Texas, she followed Charles. She wanted to know what he was doing while he was out in the streets. She watched as he got out his car and went inside the house. She waited for what seemed like forever. Unable to wait any longer, she called him on his cell. At first, he didn't pick up the phone but after calling five times, he finally answered. He only said a couple of words to her, but they were words she would never forget. "I'm home with my wife." The line went clear and that was the last straw that broke the camel's back.

The night Nancy left Texas she sent his wife a care package; pictures of her and Charles together, their family portrait they had taken, and a letter explaining to his wife of who she was. Nancy vowed that Charles would never win. He had already destroyed her and she wanted nothing but to destroy his marriage.

Nancy now living in Baltimore, had moved from one hood to another one. She had found a small two-bedroom apartment for her and Winter. It wasn't much, but it was all she could afford. Yeah, she had stolen the five hundred stacks from Charles but she didn't have a job due to the fear of being recognized by someone who knew Charles. She didn't want to blow the money.

Nancy had never worked a day in her life. Charles always took care of her. Before she met Charles, she would get funds from whatever man she was with at the moment. She never graduated from high school and didn't have plans on going back. Only plan she had was to survive in this world and to give her daughter the best she could.

# Chapter 2

Winter was chilling at Abe's house with him. She would go sit with him daily, or every other day, so he wouldn't have to be home alone. Abe's mother was a full-blown crackhead and never was home. He was being raised by his older brother, Tristin who was the head of the gang GMS. Get Money Soldiers was a gang of youngins that were uncaring and heartless. They would kill your grandmother if it involved getting money. Nobody was excluded. All of them ranged between the ages of thirteen to twenty-two. Tristin trained every member in his crew to be a cold-blooded killer.

"So what, you still thinking about joining your brother's gang?" Winter asked Abe.

"I don't want to Winter, but it's only a matter of time before he makes me join. You know how he is," Abe told her.

"But you have so many choices out here Abe, why don't you choose one? You can talk to the counselors at school or ask my mother how she can help. I already told her your situation," Winter admitted.

Abe wasn't shocked at how Winter was so empathetic to his life. In the years that they have known each other, they grew very close and he somehow fell in love with his best friend.

"Winter, just leave it alone for now, we can talk about this another time. Can we just chill, watch some TV, and do our homework before your mother comes and get you?" Abe asked.

# The Secrets He Kept

"This isn't over Abe. If something ever happened to you I wouldn't even know how to handle that." Winter shyly put her hair behind her ear.

They both sat back on the couch and finished watching TV.

"I promise you Winter, nothing will happen to me and I also promise I will make the right decision," Abe said.

At eleven years old, the love and friendship these two kids had between them could put any twenty-year-old's relationship to shame. Abraham had to grow up fast. Living in the household, with a cracked out mother and a dope-dealing killer as an older brother, Abe knew his chances at surviving in B-more were slim to none. He grew wiser and smarter, quicker than most.

In his mind, he knew if he had Winter to hold him down and keep him on the straight and narrow path, his life would turn out better than anyone in their neighborhood expected. He respected their friendship so much. Every time he was around Winter, she made him want to do better.

Abe looked at Winter and smiled and thought to his self, *I wonder does she love me the same way that I love her. But time will tell if she does; right now I don't want to scare her away.* He pushed the thoughts to the back of his head and continued to enjoy her company. As time went on, the two friends went from watching TV, to arguing over who was right or wrong on their science homework, to Abe fixing Winter a fried bologna sandwich with just only mustard and cheese. This was her favorite, and to top it off he made his famous grape Kool-Aid so she could wash it all down with.

After they both ate, they settled back down and played a game of checkers before it was time for Winter's mother to come pick her up.

"You know what Abe, I hate being the only child," Winter admitted out the blue.

"Winter, how can you be sure your father didn't have any more kids?" Abe asked her back.

"How will I find that out? My mother said he died when I was six that's why we left, and every time I ask anything about him she tells me to leave it alone."

"Do you have any pictures of him?" Abe asked.

"No, but my mother has a big box she keeps locked up tight that I am not allowed to touch," Winter said.

"Well until we are both old enough to find out who he is, consider me your brother," Abe piped.

And with that said, Abe gave Winter a big hug and gave her a triple jump to end their checker game.

"I'm going to beat you one day Abe," Winter hollered with a huge grin on her face.

"Yeah, say anything, you know you will never beat me." The two friends fell to the floor cracking up laughing, and at that moment Tristin walked in and threw his car keys on the board game they had just finished playing.

"Why every time I come home you here Winter? What y'all two doing, fucking or something?" Tristin asked to a stunned Winter.

"If you must know Tristin, we are too young to have sex so I will appreciate it if you don't talk to me like that." Abe sat there shocked at Winter's boldness to his dangerous older brother, and Tristin sat there amused too. He threw his head back, gave a hearty evil laugh, left the kids alone, and went into his bedroom.

"I don't like your brother," Winter told him.

Her whole mood had changed. She was now ready to leave and go home.

"Yeah, I know. I don't like him either but you got to not talk to him like that. You know I heard him telling Greg he killed somebody," Abe expressed.

He knew just how dangerous his brother was and wanted to warn Winter before she said something to him and gotten herself in trouble.

"I'm not scared of him and you shouldn't be either. My momma told me the only person I should be scared of is God," Winter added with much attitude.

At that very moment, Abe realized just how special Winter was and never wanted their friendship to end. He gave her a wide smile and nodded his head as if he understood her.

Tristin did like Winter. She was the only friend his brother had, but money was money and getting paid a hundred thousand dollars to kill Winter and her mother, was something he wasn't going to pass up. Tristin sat on his bed and pulled out his chrome .380 revolver he kept in a lock box under his floorboard. This was a gun he didn't mind getting rid of once he took those fatal shots that was soon to end Winter and her mother's life that night. He got dressed in all black and called his benefactor to make sure that the hit was still on.

"Yo this T!" Tristin yelled on his end on the phone.

"Look, no names on the line please; I can't let this haunt me for the rest of my life. Your money was transferred into the account in the name you gave me so you have the green light and don't call me again," his secret benefactor told him.

"Aight cool, that problem will be handled tonight," Tristin assured the caller before he heard the line go dead in his ear.

# The Secrets He Kept

Tristin poked his head out of his door and called over to his little brother.

"Yo Abe, check it out lil' man."

"What! I'm busy, I have company right now," Abe screamed back.

He was trying to stand up to him like Winter said. Impressing her was a must for him. He wanted to show her just how much talking to her mean to him and that he was listening.

"Lil' bitch ass nigga, get yo' prissy ass over here and see what I want," Tristin hollered back getting frustrated.

Abraham walked over to his brother with his chest held high. Even though his brother disrespected him from time to time, Abe knew the love he had for him was endless. In his eyes, he was just trying to make him tougher so he could get through his childhood to make it into manhood. So Abraham didn't have to make the mistakes he did, or even get hooked on that crack shit like their father did before he left.

"What man, I'm busy and her mother is on her way to get her any minute," Abe huffed.

"Aww man, that's all I wanted to see, was what time she was going home. I got business to handle in here before your mother decides she wants to pop up," Tristin lied.

"You know dang gone well Tracie ain't gone bring her butt in here no time soon," Abe replied with a confused look on his face.

"Well aight Abe, when my peoples show up make sure you show her to the door." Tristin slammed his cracked door in Abe's face and went back to what he was doing.

Abraham went back to Winter and sat next to her. "You want to play another round before your mother shows up?" he asked.

"No, while you were talking to your brother, she called me and said she will be here at your door in a minute. I'll call you tonight to let you know you was wrong on the science homework." Winter gathered her belongings.

"I wouldn't expect anything less from you Winter. Anything less." Abe shook his head and helped her put her things together, when a knock came at the door.

They got up off the floor and he walked her to his front door and opened it.

Nancy was standing there with a worried look on her face and bags under her eyes.

"You ready Winter?" Nancy questioned.

"Yes ma'am," she responded back. She turned to her best friend and waved her hand goodbye when she walked out.

As they walked towards their house, she turned to see Abe still standing in his doorway and hollered "I'll call you when I get home." Winter gave him one last wave before he stepped back inside his house.

# Chapter 3

Nancy had been gone all day with a friend. She was always trying to come up with ways to make some money. She had found a place that was hiring folks to work from home, which was right up her alley. That way she wouldn't have to be away from Winter. She made small talk with her daughter on their short walk home.

"How was your day?" Nancy asked her.

"It was nice mom, Abe and I did all of our homework he fixed me something to eat and we played checkers. He always beats me in checkers," Winter told her mom.

"That's good baby. Has his mother came back home?" Nancy probed.

"No, but his brother came home so he won't be home alone tonight," Winter reveled.

"I think he is in a bad situation and I need to do something about it," Nancy muttered.

"Like what ma?" Winter cut her eyes up at her mother.

"Maybe report it to CPS or even the school, on how he is living," Nancy answered.

"Ma, please don't do that! They will take him away and I will never see him again," Winter whined.

"Winter Ann, that boy needs help. I got to do something. He can't keep living like that. I don't feel conformable letting you go over there with all that's going on," Nancy snapped.

"Ma, please, just don't tell anybody. I will start having him come over to the house if that makes you feel better," Winter cried.

"What is it with you and this boy?" Nancy stopped walking.

She placed her hands on her hips and waited for an answer. It was time for her to get to the bottom of things.

"He is the only friend I got. Besides him, I have nobody. You're trying to take that away from me," Winter pouted.

She let her tears roll down her face. She felt like her world was crashing.

"I'm not trying to take him away from you honey. I'm just trying to help him," Nancy explained.

"Ma, I promise it's going to get better for him. His brother told him tonight he was going to be home more," Winter lied.

"Oh really?" Nancy looked at her daughter sideways.

"Yeah, that's what we were talking about before you came over to get me," Winter added.

"Ok that's good. Well it seems like I don't have to do anything," Nancy said.

Winter was glad she'd gotten Abe out of that one. She wipe her tears away and smiled on the inside. She was sure going to talk to him about it tonight when she got home. One thing she was glad her mother didn't know was Tristin was in a gang. Nancy would flip her wig if she ever found out about that.

They continued the walk home which wasn't far. They made some more small talk about both of their days. Nancy was a great mother and loved the relationship she had with Winter. She had seen a big change in her daughter and thought it was time she really found out what really happened with her father. Over the years she had told lie after lie to cover up the real reason they had to move.

Nancy unlocked the apartment door and let Winter in. "Go take a bath and if you got any more homework get it done," Nancy instructed.

"Yes ma'am," Winter went upstairs, ran straight to her room and closed her door.

"And don't stay on that damn phone long," Nancy yelled.

One thing Nancy knew was Winter was already dialing Abe's number. The two acted like they couldn't be apart from each other for a second. She laughed because she knew the feeling. Her daughter was in love. At their age, love was something young kids didn't know about but Winter and Abe's friendship was different.

Nancy headed straight to the kitchen to get dinner started. She made something quick that only took her an hour to make: spaghetti and meatballs with garlic bread. After dinner was done she went and got in the shower as well.

The front door swung open and the man walked in. He closed the door behind him quietly. He looked around the room and listened for sounds. He could hear the shower running from where he was standing at the bottom of the stairs. He glided up the stairs and walked towards the running water. He was startled by the talking coming from behind a room door across the hall. He walked toward the voice. He got to Winter's room and placed his hand on the doorknob. He turned the knob and started opening the door. He was stopped in his tracks by the sound of the water stopping. Thinking quick on his feet, he retreated to the hallway closet.

\*\*\*

Meanwhile back at Abe's house, he was on the phone with Winter. "For real?"

"Yeah, I lied to her about your brother said he was going to be home more so she said she won't call the people," Winter whispered not wanting her mother to hear her.

"That's good. I'm glad you thought quickly," Abe informed her.

"Boy you know I got yo' back. We just got to make sure we stick to that story so she won't get suspicious," Winter muttered.

"You right. Thanks again too. If she had called them people I don't know what they would have done or where I would be," Abe thought aloud.

"Yeah, I know." Winter added.

"Did you get a chance to go back over the science homework?" Abe changed the subject.

"No, I'm going to take a bath first. I rushed in here to call you first before I forgot," Winter admitted.

"Ok, you go ahead and do that. Tristin is in there yelling my name like the house is on fire. I guess his lil' meeting is about to start so let me go listen to what they talking 'bout and I will call you before I go to bed," Abe murmured.

"Listen to their meeting? Abe, are you joining that gang tonight?" Winter muttered.

"No, but every time he has one of his lil' meetings, he wants me in the room. Hold on," Abe told her. "What?" he yelled. "I will be there in a minute dang," he huffed before he placed the receiver to his ear. "Aye, I got to go. I will call you after they leave," Abe said.

"Ok. I know my moms is going to be coming in here in a minute. She done cooked and we always have to eat dinner together," Winter complained.

"You already ate though," Abe confirmed.

"I know and I told her that, but you already know how she is so let me go and I will be waiting on your call," Winter concluded.

"Ok bye," Abe said.

"It's not bye it's see you later or talk to you later," Winter corrected.

"Hey, I've been meaning to ask you where you get that from?" Abe questioned.

"Off that one movie we watch last week at your house, *John Q*," Winter giggled.

"Oh ok, well, talk to you later because I hear Tristin walking this way." Abe stood up off his bedroom floor.

"Ok, I will be waiting," Winter laughed before she hung up the phone.

"Boy I know good and well you hear me calling you," Tristin scolded as soon as he opened the room door.

"I heard you, geesh. I was on the phone," Abe yelled back.

"Who the fuck you think you talking to?" Tristin rushed him.

Tristin jacked Abe up by his shirt and slammed him against the wall. "You better watch your tone with me."

Abe huffed and puffed, mad cause of the way his brother was treating him. He would be glad when he got older and able to control his own life.

"Now it's time to make a man out of you. Playing time is over. Let's go," Tristin barked and turned on his heels walking away, leaving Abe with his thoughts.

# The Secrets He Kept

Abe straightened up his shirt and took a couple of deep breaths. He walked into the dining room where the crew was seated. He looked around at all the many faces of GMS. There were young ones and older ones. He even saw a familiar face he hadn't seen in a while. A kid that use to be the third wheel with him and Winter. The boy had stopped coming to school and then Abe heard the boy's house burned down. He never asked were the boy had gone after that. He stood back and watched his brother take over the meeting.

"Ok, now that everybody is here except for Greg, we can get started. We got two hits that need our attention tonight. One is easy. Terrance, Luke, Bam, and Leon, y'all can take that one. Go ahead and have a seat in the front room and Mike will come give y'all the particulars," Tristin instructed.

He waited until they were all gone. That only left Tristin, Abe, and Jon in the room.

"Now that they are gone, Abe is new to the crew and I want him in on this job. I think it's time he learn how to man up." Tristin laughed an evil laugh.

"Bout damn time you brought lil' man in on the action," Jon stated.

"But I don't want to be a part of y'all crew. I've been talking to Winter-"

"You talked to Winter about what? I hope you not telling that damn girl my muthafucking business!" Tristin interrupted.

"No I didn't tell nothing 'bout what you do, dang," Abe lied.

Winter was Abe's friend and he told her everything. She was the only person in this world he could talk to without being judged.

"Enough about that damn girl. Your soft ass needs to be thinking about getting money and not that crush of yours," Tristin hollered.

"She is not a crush. That's my friend and she cares more about me then you ever did," Abe hissed.

"We will see after tonight. Your ass is in because I say so. I don't wanna hear no more about it. You are now a part of GMS so act like it," Tristin screamed.

Abe mumbled something under his breath and crossed his arms across his chest. He didn't like being forced into a gang. But what was it for him to do but to go along with it. If he didn't, he knew Tristin would get violent.

"Ok brah, what's the job?" Jon tried to defuse the situation.

"Greg snagged this one. His peoples back in Texas wants someone touched here in the city. The pay is one hundred stacks. We will split it four ways," Tristin explained.

"Four ways?" Jon questioned.

"Yeah, Greg, Abe, me and you," Tristin stated.

"Hold on a minute. If that nigga getting a cut shouldn't he be here for the meeting? I don't care if it was his people who called in the order," Jon piped.

"Nigga shut the hell up and chill. Greg is already on the job. He's been watching the target since earlier. He will call us once the coast is clear so we can move," Tristin growled.

"Oh ok. Go on then," Jon smiled.

"The target is on two people, a woman and a child. The benefactor wants both killed and then the house burnt down. They don't want the bodies found," Tristin went on.

"Oh my God! You guys are going to kill a kid? Tristin, I don't want any parts of this," Abe cried.

# The Secrets He Kept

He began to walk away only to be stopped by an evil look from his brother. He couldn't believe his ears. He now knew his brother was a monster. The kind of monsters his teacher taught him about.

"Too late. You already in so shut up and listen closely," Tristin screamed.

"Maybe we shouldn't let lil man be in on this one," Jon muttered.

He was thinking of more money for him.

"Nawl, he has to. This one is special and he has to be the one to pull the trigger." Tristin looked at Abe.

"But we throwing him in on some heavy shit. I think we should ease him in on a lighter job," Jon added.

"Fuck that. This is the perfect job for him," Tristin stated.

Abe was speechless. He was trying to talk but no words came out for some reason. The whole conversation was playing in his head and he just couldn't get over the fact his brother wanted him to kill a kid. "Why me?" Abe finally spoke.

He was trembling from the inside out.

"Because the target is someone... let's say someone you know and you know the layout of the house like the back of your hands. When we get there you will show us were to go and then we will tie the targets up. It will be your responsibility to pull the trigger," Tristin ordered.

"Why I got to shoot somebody though? I can't do it. I just can't," Abe ranted.

"Because I said so and you will or I will kill you. This is the only way in the gang. Blood in, blood out," Tristin said calmly but his look was one of a true killer.

Abe saw the look and didn't say a word. He had never seen his brother act this way and it scared the shit out of him. "Who, who... I mean you said I know them, who is it?"

"Hmm. Now this is where it gets good at. Seems like I'm not the only one that doesn't like your lil' friend Winter. Somebody is paying big money to have her and her mother killed," Tristin evilly laughed.

"Ah man. T, I don't think lil' man should do this for real. That's a lil too much for him." Jon was serious this time.

After hearing what the job was he was sure of it; this job wasn't one Abe should be on. He had seen Abe and Winter interact together so he knew just how close they were.

"Nooooo! Please don't do it. Not her. Tristin, I've never asked you for anything but please don't do it. I will be good and listen to what you say. Please," Abe cried.

His heart was hurting something serious. He felt like all the air was being sucked out of his body. The room began to spin. He had to sit down. Abe slid his body down the wall and brought his head to his knees.

"Look at him crying like a lil' bitch. Suck that shit up. The hit has been made and we got to do this," Tristin laughed.

Abe closed his eyes and said a prayer. He couldn't believe his ears. Was his brother telling him that he had to kill his best friend? How could that be? Abe was feeling sick. He hopped up off the floor and ran to the bathroom. He had held his vomit long enough. Hugging the rim of the toilet, he released everything he had inside of him. As he vomited he also released a few sorrowful tears.

# Chapter 4

Greg stood in the hallway closet, pulled his phone out his jacket pocket and sent Tristin a text informing him he was in place, and to be on their way. He peeked out from time to time to see if his targets decided to do anything to ruin their plans. If he had to, he was going to kill them his self. He was having thoughts about having fun with Winter's sexy ass mother. His aunt told him to make sure she felt the most pain and he was gone make sure she did. The targets were in the kitchen eating when he got a text saying that they were outside and ready to bust that move.

Greg crept downstairs and peeked around the corner, where Winter and Nancy were still sitting at their kitchen table eating and laughing. He slowly opened up the door and let Tristin, Abe and Jon in. He signaled towards the kitchen to let them know that the targets were in there. Tristin gave him some dap, grabbed his brother and then led him towards the kitchen. Abe tried to fight but he was no match against his brother. Tristin gave him a back handed slap that landed against Abe's face hard.

"Either you do this or I kill you myself lil' bro, it won't make me any difference," Tristin stated to his younger brother.

Abe wiped his bleeding mouth with his shirt and with tears falling feverishly down his face, he poked his chest out as far as it would go and he followed his big brother into the lion's den. The four men walked into the kitchen with black masks on their face and startled Winter and her mom.

"How the hell did y'all get in my house?" Nancy asked, as she jumped from her seat and went to grab a frightened Winter to protect her from the intruders.

"Has anyone ever told you to keep your doors locked? This is a bad neighborhood you live in," Tristin said before reaching over and separating Nancy from her crying daughter.

"Look, if you just leave now, I have at least twenty thousand you can walk out of here with. Just leave my daughter out of this. Please, I beg of you!" Nancy pleaded with her attacker.

"Tell you what... you show me where you got twenty stacks at and I'll make it my business to make your death quick," Tristin said before he snatched Nancy up and pulled her out of her kitchen kicking and screaming.

"PLEASE! Don't hurt my baby," Nancy screamed out while she was being drug up her stairs by the roots of her hair.

"Shut the fuck up." Tristin smacked her hard against her face with his gun, giving Nancy a huge gash on her forehead that started to bleed profusely.

Greg followed Tristin up the stairs and helped him tie Nancy up to her bed. They stripped her butt naked and taped her mouth shut. Greg took off his mask, sat next to Nancy and rubbed her inner thigh with his pistol. Tristin took his off as well, and proceeded to follow Greg's lead.

"So where is this twenty grand I've been hearing so much about?" Greg asked while he slowly inserted the pistol inside of Nancy's pussy.

Nancy mumbled incoherently under her taped mouth, before Tristin snatched it off so she could speak.

"If I tell you where it's at, can you promise me my daughter will be left alone?" Nancy tried to plead for Winter's life once again.

She knew her life was gone already and that was something she could deal with.

"You have my word," Tristin lied.

"There is a box that is locked under my bed, it's in there. The combination is 0742," Nancy said before Greg smacked her again across the head with his pistol, knocking her out this time.

Tristin went under her bed, pulled out the box and unlocked it. When he opened it up, he saw pictures of a six-year-old Winter, her mother and a man holding her, and the twenty grand she spoke about. *So the bitch wasn't lying,* Tristin thought to his self.

Greg looked inside the box as well before pushing it on the floor, and then he went and stood over Nancy's unconscious body. He begin unzipping his pants anticipating sliding up in her. He pulled out his erect penis and put a conJarrett on. He slapped Nancy a couple times so she could wake up. When Nancy came to, she saw what her attacker planned to do with her. Not one tear fell from her face. She wasn't going to give them the satisfaction of seeing her break down. Her only thought was that she hoped her daughter's fate was better than hers was.

Greg and Tristin untied her and laid her face down on the bed. They both took turns raping her with their dick and guns. With every stroke, Nancy pleaded with them to stop and to let her go. At that moment, her pride went out the window. Fear and pain was all she felt. After raping her viciously in her ass, pussy, and mouth, Greg finally pissed all over her.

The men laughed at the sight of their handy work.

"Damn that bitch got some good pussy," Tristin piped as he pulled his pants up.

"Too bad she got to die," Greg joined.

He slid his manhood back in his pants as well. He grabbed his pistol off the foot of the bed, ready to finish the job.

"Please just leave us alone," Nancy whispered.

She was in too much pain to talk any louder than she was.

Tristin pulled out a bottle of lighter fluid and emptied the entire bottle over her body and her room.

"Let's go finish this shit and get out of here," Tristin replied once he was finished.

Greg aimed and without a blink of the eye, he put two bullets in the back of her head.

Tristin walked out the room with Greg on his heels. One part of their plan was over; it was time to get the last part done. Greg made a pit stop to flush the condoms down the toilet. He wanted to make sure he didn't leave that behind.

Abe stood in the corner of the kitchen far away from his best friend, with a mask on his face but his head down. While Jon had a gun placed to Winter's head, he cried silently and made sure not to speak so she wouldn't recognize his voice. He was beyond devastated about what his brother planned to do. He wanted to help Winter, but he wasn't a match for one guy let alone three guys. Greg and Tristin came back to the kitchen with their masks back on and got straight to business.

"Since we ended that party early upstairs, maybe this can be the after party," Tristin joked with the guys in the room. Everyone laughed except Winter and Abe.

"Where is my mom?" Winter asked with tears clouding her vision.

She was scared shitless. All she wanted was her mother. She had heard the loud noise but refused to believe her mom was already dead.

"Oh baby girl, you don't have to worry about that, you will see her soon," Greg uttered.

"Can I see her? Can I go to her?" Winter pleaded with the masked men. "Ma!" Winter called for her.

Her tears flowed heavily.

"Look, I know you sick bastards are having fun but can we get this over with? We have other business to tend to tonight," Jon interrupted the fun and games.

He wasn't feeling raping a ten year old.

"Aight, now for the main event," Tristin told his friends.

He grabbed Abe and put the gun in his hand. "This is your show, now hurry up and get it over with so we can get the fuck up out of here." Tristin stood back and watched.

Abe stood there with a wet mask due to his crying, and a shaky hand due to the act he was about to commit. The gun felt like it weighed a ton, but he managed to pull it up and point it at Winter. "I'm so sorry," Abe whispered.

He said a silent prayer, right before he closed his eyes and pulled the trigger wildly until it just clicked. The room was silent and nobody said a word. When he opened his eyes, all he could see was his best friend, his only friend he had, body riddled with bullets, fall next to Jon's feet. He walked over to Winter, closed her eyes and kissed her on her forehead. He dropped the gun next to her body and walked out of Winter's house not looking back.

Greg, Jon and Tristin couldn't be more proud of their new team member. Jon pulled out the second bottle of lighter fluid dousing the house down. He worked his way from room to room until he got back to the living room.

"Y'all niggas ready?" Jon hollered.

"Let's get the fuck up out of here," Tristin ordered.

The men made their way to the door and Jon ran up the stairs. He lit a match and watched the flames start to dance up the walls. In a matter of seconds, the room was engulfed with flames and he could hear Nancy's body frying. They all ran out the house heading to their car which was parked a block over.

Tristin made it to the car first. He heard Abe but hadn't put his eyes on him. He walked around the car and there he was, sitting in the grass crying his eyes out.

"Man, get your dumb ass in the car," Tristin barked.

He hopped in the car and started the engine. Jon and Greg had got to the car just in time. They all piled in the car and was on their way.

Abe couldn't do anything but watch how the flames was starting to grow. The windows in the upstairs bedroom started to crack and neighbors were coming out their houses trying to see what was going on. Abe pulled his mask off his face. He was in pain at the thought of the fire ripping through Winter's body. The longer he sat and watched the scene play out, the more he gained courage.

Abe opened the car door and jumped out while the car was still in motion. He hit the ground hard but bounced back up in a matter of minutes. He stood in the middle of the street and watched to see if the car would stop but they kept going. The police and fire department sirens could be heard in the distance and would be there shortly. Abe had a little time left to get Winter out the house. He had to try at least. He took off running towards the burning house. His heart wouldn't let him just leave her like that.

# The Secrets He Kept

Abe walked in the front door and grab the doorknob. It was hot as shit and he burnt his hand.

"Young man, get away from that door," a neighbor hollered at him.

"I got to save my friend. She's in here, I can't," Abe yelled back as he took off his jacket.

He wrapped it around his hand and attempted to open the door again. This time he gained access only to be hit in the face by the heat. He fought against the smoke to get to the kitchen. When he entered, he put a towel in some cold water and tied it around his face. He grabbed Winter by her shoulders and dragged her out the back door. He checked to see if she had a pulse and there wasn't. In a panic, he picked her head up and laid it in his lap. He begin talking to her. "Winter I'm sorry. Please don't die on me." Crying and begging, he felt for her pulse again. This time he took his time searching for one. He found one; it was a faint pulse but he could still feel it. Relieved, he placed her head on the ground gently and prepared to leave. Abe left her there and ran as fast as he could. He knew he had to get out of there. He opened his phone and dialed 911.

"911 what's your emergency?" the operator asked.

"There is a house on fire and I think the people in there are trapped," Abe yelled into his phone, still running at full speed.

"Can I have the address sir?" The operator replied.

"9214 Wickermore Drive, please hurry!" Abe yelled out of breath.

"The officers are on the way already. Can you stay on the line until they arrive?" the operator said.

Abe cut the call short, threw his phone on the ground and never looked back. He felt better knowing the sirens he heard were coming to see about Winter.

# The Secrets He Kept

# Chapter 5

The Baltimore fire department and the police arrived on the scene in no time. The house was engulfed in flames now as they tried to control the blaze. A fire fighter stormed through the back of the house almost tripping over Winter's body. He spoke into his walkie-talkie.

"Over! We have a body here! It's a female looks to be between ten to thirteen, send a paramedic now. Over!" The paramedics rushed to Winter's side and checked her pulse to see if she was breathing.

Again, it was faint, but they got straight to work. The paramedic inserted an IV in her arm and a neck brace on her neck. He then placed an oxygen mask on her face to get more oxygen in her lungs. Once she was secure and her vitals were stable, they carefully loaded her on a gurney and whisked her off to the ambulance. They secured her and then pulled off immediately. On their way to Greater Baltimore Medical Center, Winter's vitals crashed three times.

The medics tried their best to keep her stable, but it seemed like everything they did didn't work. They were only a few feet from the hospital, when things took a turn for the worst. Winter crashed again right before they turned into the emergency room entrance. The ambulance stopped abruptly and rushed Winter into the emergency room at full speed.

"We have a Code Blue, a little African American child between the ages of ten to thirteen, possible smoke inhalations and I counted four bullet wounds. We just lost a pulse. It's not looking good," the paramedic said to a nurse and doctor who rushed over to Winter's aid.

Winter was rushed into surgery. The doctors worked on her for what seemed like all night. They would stop the bleeding in one spot and then move to another one. One by one, the doctor removed bullets from Winter's frail body.

"Hold it! We can't keep going. We have already had this body opened for ten hours. Let's close her up. We will have to go back in another day," the doctor order as he began to close her up.

It took him another hour or so to get Winter closed up and heavily sedated. She was left on a respirator and wasn't breathing on her own. The doctor's felt she had lost too much blood and didn't want to stand the chance of losing her all together. Winter was placed in a medically induced coma.

"Where are her parents?" the doctor asked a nurse.

"Doctor Cole, her mother died in the fire tonight," the nurse explained to him.

"Are the officers still here?" Doctor Cole questioned.

"No sir, they left a long time ago, but the lead Detective gave me his card and wants you to call him," the nurse replied.

Doctor Cole took the card. "Thanks Tammy."

"You welcome doctor," Tammy added.

Doctor Cole walked away tucking the card in his pocket. He had a long day and needed a smoke. He made a mental note to give the detective a call.

Doctor Cole took his break and the only thing on his mind was the young girl he had just finished working on. His heart goes out to her. He was kind of glad the girl was in a coma. How could he explain to her that her mother was dead? Now he had his work cut out for him. The next of kin needed to be contacted, but he had to start by finding out what the girl's name was. He put his cigarette out and walked back in to his office.

"Baltimore Police Department, how can I help you?" the secretary's bubbly voice echoed through the phone.

"Um yes, is Detective Gonzales in?" Doctor Cole calmly spoke.

"Yes he is. Hold please," the secretary responded and placed the call on hold.

Doctor Cole waited for Detective Gonzales to come to the phone. There was a slight pause before he heard a voice.

"Detective Gonzales."

"Um yes sir. This is Doctor Cole from Greater Baltimore Medical Center," Doctor Cole announced.

"Oh hey. I tried to wait around for you to get out of surgery. How did it go?" Detective Gonzales asked.

"Ten hours and we still have to remove two more bullets. The child is now in a coma," Doctor Cole revealed.

"You think she will pull through?" Detective Gonzales questioned.

He needed this information. By the looks of things back at the house, it could have been a double homicide if she didn't pull through.

"Right now it's touch and go. She lost a lot of blood and there is swelling around her brain. My medical opinion is if she does she may lose all memory but we will see. We won't know until she wakes up," Doctor Cole told him.

"Do you still have the bullets you removed?" Detective Gonzales muttered.

"Of course," Doctor Cole replied back.

"Good, I will be by there a little later to pick those up for ballistics," Detective Gonzales told him.

"That will be fine. I have a question for you, if you don't mind," Doctor Cole informed him.

"Go ahead, shoot," Detective Gonzales responded.

"Have you guys been able to contact anybody in this child's family? She was brought in with nothing. Not even a name. I was told her mother died in the fire but I would like to contact a family member to let them know she is here and still alive," Doctor Cole ranted.

"As a matter of fact we haven't. We canvased the neighborhood and everyone that we talked to and knew the victims, states they were here alone. No other family in the state," Detective Gonzales remarked.

"Do you guys have a name for her?" Doctor Cole asked.

"At this moment we are not revealing that. We are afraid that whoever did this will return and finish the job," Detective Gonzales disclosed.

"I can understand that. For right now we will name her Cherish Doe. I will let you go and will see you when you come back by," Doctor Cole prepared to end his call.

He could see he wasn't getting anywhere with the Detective.

"Ok bye," Detective Gonzales replied before hanging up the phone.

***

Meanwhile, Abe had watched the ambulance as it left Winter's block. From where he was standing, he could still see the flames. The fire was so big the fire fighters could only contain the blaze. Abe continued his walk home. He knew his brother was pissed but he didn't care; he had to try to make it right.

Abe walked into the house only to be covered with darkness. He fumbled around in the house until he reached the light switch. Once the light invaded the room, he could see it clear.

"Tristin you here?" Abe yelled out.

There was more silence. Abe walked into his bedroom. He walked to the phone and picked it up but stopped in his tracks. The call he was going to make was to his best friend. "Fuck!" Abe screamed and hauled the phone across the room out of frustration. The phone hit the wall and shattered into many pieces.

Abe laid in his bed and cried a river. He cried from his soul. He had never in his eleven years of living felt the pain he was feeling. His cries were so loud they could be heard from across the street. Abe cried so long he now had a headache. He got up from his bed and went in the bathroom. He opened the medicine cabinet and searched it. There was nothing but roaches and cobwebs. He slammed the door shut and walked into the front room. He laid on the couch and stared at the clock. The clock said it was after four in the morning.

Abe laid and thought about his actions. He wanted better for his self. He closed his eyes and opened his mouth. This time he wanted to speak to God out loud. "God, if you help me out of this situation I promise I will do better. I'm so sorry for what I have done God and hope you can forgive me. Please save Winter. If you do this for me I promise I will never do wrong again. God, please order my steps and lead me in the right direction. Amen."

Abe closed his eye and rolled over. Sleep over took him in a matter of minutes. He had been sleep for a while but was jolted out of his sleep by a hard lick up side his head.

"Get your punk ass up!" Tristin screamed throwing Abe on the floor.

# The Secrets He Kept

Abe was afraid to open his eyes. He hit the ground hard and the wind was knocked out of him. He rolled over and was stopped by Tristin's goons. Before Abe knew what hit him, he had too many hands to count being thrown at him. Abe curled up in a fetal position and tried his best to cover her face. The goons were raining blows at him so fast he couldn't keep up. He could hear Tristin in the back ground yelling.

"Fuck him up!" Tristin coached.

He was pissed beyond measure with his brother's actions. "Lil mothafucka almost fucked up my money."

Tristin didn't care that his brother was only eleven. He was going to make a man out of him yet. When it came to his money, anybody could get it. His momma was a prime example. She had stolen some money from him and hadn't been back since. He spent most of his days and nights looking for her. He had something real nice planned for her as well.

Tristin saw Abe was now bleeding all over the floor. It excited him at the sight and he joined in. "Stupid mothafucka almost got us caught!" Tristin hollered.

He stood back and watched a little while longer. He could see his brother was no longer moving. "Enough!"

All the goons stopped mid swing. Some were breathing heavily and others who was putting in hella work, was sweating. Tristin nudged Abe with his foot and he still didn't move.

"Oh shit, y'all niggas done killed him!" Tristin's voice got caught in his throat.

Tristin wanted to teach his brother a lesson not kill him. He didn't realize it but he was now holding his breathe.

"That lil nigga isn't dead. His chest is moving," Jon stated from the door.

He didn't agree with Tristin having the goons give Abe a beating. He tried to tell Tristin that Abe wasn't going to be to handle the job but he didn't listen to him.

Tristin watched Abe's chest long and hard. He confirmed it was true. Abe's chest was still moving. He breathes a sigh of relief. "He ain't dead but his ass will feel it when he do wake up."

"You ain't going to put the lil' nigga in the bed?" Jon asked.

"Nawl, fuck him. Let's get up out of here and go spend this money." With that Tristin walked out the house with his goons in tow.

# Chapter 6

Tristin left his brother unconscious on the bedroom floor, without a single thought or remorse in his body. Him and his goons got into his Chevy Impala and cruised the streets of B-more, a hundred thousand dollars richer. He pulled out his phone and made a call to his benefactor.

"Yo it's me. The two little birdies flew away after I opened the cage up. We won't have any more problems with them," Tristin stated on his end of the phone.

"Are you sure they flew away? Are you positive it's done? Did you see it for yourself?" his benefactor babbled.

She was excited the job was done and it wouldn't come back to haunt her.

"Yeah, I watched them fly all the way to heaven. If you need anything else you know how to get in contact with me or your peeps." Tristin laughed before he heard his line go dead.

Tristin closed his burner phone, rolled down the window and threw it out on the side of the road. He had no use for it anymore. After every job he would get a new phone and number.

Rachel Crosby closed her phone and laid her restless body down on her California king-sized bed. She had been waiting on this day for five years and this phone call for two weeks. She sat up on her huge bed and split her phone in half. She walked over to the fireplace and threw it in. She never had anyone killed before; hell, she wasn't even a fighter in real life.

# The Secrets He Kept

Rachel thought back to the day that change her life. It was a rainy Saturday morning and she'd ran to her mailbox in her silk robe with an umbrella over her head. She grabbed her mail which contained a manila envelope and some bills. She ran back to the house so she didn't mess up her nice robe Charles had just purchased for her. She walked in the house removing her rain boots and jacket.

Rachel sat on her white Italian leather couch and cuddled up with her pillows. She opened up her bills first so she could get them out the way. After writing checks to cover the light and gas bills, she picked up the strange manila envelope that had her name on it with no return address.

Rachel opened it up and pulled out the contents. Her heart skipped several beats. One by one, she looked through the pictures of her husband and some woman holding a little girl. She read the note that had the heading of 'A Scorned Mistress'. It told her how the woman and Charles had a relationship half the time that they been married, and that the child he was holding in the pictures was his daughter Winter. The letter also said that the only reason she was coming forward was because Charles was lying to both of them. She let the words of the letter play over in her head.

Rachel let the photos and letter fall to her feet. She was shocked about finding out about yet another affair her husband was having. This affair was one she just couldn't overlook. There was a child involved. She threw her head back on the couch and gently massaged her temples. She could feel her heart break as if a glass shattered on the floor. Rage, anger, and grief clouded her thoughts all at the same time. She lifted up her head, pulled her robe tightly around her shapely body, and went to the bar she had fully stocked.

Pulling out a bottle of Don Julio tequila, she needed a drink. No ice, water, or chaser was needed at that time. She cracked opened the bottle, threw the top half way across her front room and downed the tequila. Now Rachel wasn't a drinker and as much as she gagged on the tart liquid, it didn't stop her from chugging out the broken bottle. Words couldn't explain what she felt.

Rachel had been with Charles her entire life, they were childhood sweethearts. Cheating was one thing but having a baby outside of the marriage was a death sentence, especially since she couldn't have kids. She knew Charles wanted kids and they recently decided to adopt. Now she was deriving a conclusion; all those nights out with the guys, handling business, all those nights he started fights and stayed out all night long. He would leave her there wrecking her brain wondering was he ok. *He did that so he could be with his other family, the family that should not have existed,* Rachel thought to herself.

Rachel took another long drink out of the bottle before smashing it on the floor. Then she smashed her wedding picture of them that was sitting on the bar. So enraged she began throwing everything she could get her hands on. Unable to contain her feelings, she started screaming at the top of her lungs and tumbling on the floor in the shattered glass. She kicked wildly and threw a tantrum like a five-year-old child.

"Ugh! You stupid motherfucker! I hate you. Why you keep doing this to me?"

Rachel's life fell apart in that moment. In her eyes, Charles, his mistress, and child was not going to beat her. She had already won the battle; she wore the ring, she had the house, and she had Charles' heart. *The only thing this bitch has is the child,* Rachel thought to herself. Rachel gathered herself up off the floor but she forgot glass was scattered everywhere and a couple of shards pierced her hands. Rachel walked into the kitchen and grabbed a towel to wrap her hand in. The pain turned into pleasure. A smile crept across her face as a crazy thought ran through her head.

After throwing a pity party for herself, she finally got her thoughts together. She had wifely duties to get done. Opening the fridge, she pulled out what she was going to make for dinner tonight. Then she quickly grabbed a huge trash bag, her dust pan, and broom and headed into the living room to clean up the mess that she had made.

Once the glass was cleaned up and the house was restored back to normal, she sat on her couch and neatly stacked the photos with the letter on the coffee table right next to her other mail. Feeling drained mentally and physically, she laid down and took a quick nap before it was time for her to get dressed and fixed dinner. Later that night, Charles walked inside his home and the aroma of a home-cooked meal filled his nostrils.

"Hey baby, I'm home, where are you? You got the house smelling wonderful," Charles screamed throughout his house, searching for his wife.

"Hey honey, I am in the kitchen putting the food on the table," Rachel screamed back.

Charles followed the scent of food and the sound of his beautiful wife's voice into his kitchen. He stepped inside the kitchen and admired how sexy his wife looked in her fitted seven jeans with a black see-through top. He slowly walked over to his wife and slid both of his arms around her waist and nuzzled his face in the crease of her neck.

Since Nancy and Winter had left Texas, he was now coming home early. It was strange at first for Charles. He felt he had given his all to Nancy and she just took it away. She left him empty. Now he was going to focus all of his love towards being with Rachel.

"You smell fantastic baby," Charles stated as he let her scent invade his senses.

"Thanks baby, now go get washed up for dinner, it's already ready so hurry up," Rachel said as she turned around in his arms and gave him a passionate kiss.

She pushed him off of her playfully and Charles turned on his heels then walked away to get ready for dinner. Rachel set the dinner mats at her kitchen dinette set since this wasn't a formal dinner. She wanted to be in a small space to deal with what she was going through. She waited for Charles to enter and start feasting on his meal.

Rachel had cooked meat loaf, garlic mash potatoes, and a garden salad. She grabbed a glass of red wine, crossed her legs, and took a sip of the sweet liquid. As tears formed in her eyes, she quickly wiped them away before he came back in the room. She could smell his Dolce and Gabbana cologne lingering outside of the kitchen so she knew he was on his way in.

"It smells heavenly baby. You out did yourself tonight, you must miss daddy," Charles spoke as he entered the kitchen and sat down at the table.

"Of course I missed you but I didn't do anything special Charles. You are my husband and I love you, this is my job," Rachel said coldly.

Charles stared at his wife and finally noticed that she was a little distant. She was acting weird but he shook it off and continued with his conversation, changing the subject. "How was your day? Did you do anything exciting today?"

Rachel only answered with one word answers. "Fine and no," she sighed.

# The Secrets He Kept

Charles chopped it up and kept eating his food. When he finished his food and saw she hadn't even touched her plate, Charles became suspicious. He wiped his mouth then walked to the sink and dropped his plate hard. He hated when his wife acted like a spoiled brat. These were the times he wished he were over there with Nancy and Winter. He had watched Nancy leave out that night with his daughter. He didn't stop her just for the simple fact that he couldn't give Nancy what she was looking for. He knew in his heart that he was holding her back from true love, so he let her go with ease. He watched her leave with his only daughter and vowed to always keep tabs on them, to make sure Winter was straight throughout her life.

*I wonder how they are doing?* Charles thought to his self.

Charles walked to his couch and turned on the TV so he didn't have to entertain Rachel's bullshit. Now he was regretting coming home so early. Rachel watched her husband with evil eyes. In moments, he would know how much pain and hatred she had inside her. She sipped on her wine and with one hand she swiped her plate of food on the floor. She rose up and walked towards her husband in the living room. She stood over him patting her foot and Charles looked up at her with irritated eyes, and kept flicking through channels trying not to start an argument.

"Charles, is there anything you need to tell me?" Rachel said with her arms folded across her chest and her glass of wine still in her hand.

"Om no. Why are you tripping?" Charles huffed.

"You sure?" Rachel probed.

"Woman, I don't feel like going through the motions with you right now so if you have something to say just fucking say it," Charles responded back.

# The Secrets He Kept

"Nawl, I'm not tripping, but I know you hiding something. I'm not going to ask you again," Rachel hissed.

"Look, I don't have anything to tell you. I haven't done anything so there is nothing to tell. Now can you please move so I can watch TV?" Charles barked.

Rachel cut her eyes to the coffee table and Charles followed her eyes. His eyes landed on the mail. He picked the mail up and skimmed through it. He came upon the photos and letter. His heart skipped a beat. With his big doe eyes, Charles scanned through the photos and read Nancy's letter. After the shock of seeing his infidelity in living color, he put his head down and tried to reach for his wife. Rachel pushed her husband away from her and took a step back.

"Why Charles? Why? I gave you twenty years of my fucking life! I never even gave another man a second glance. You were all I needed, all I ever craved for. I loved you with my entire soul and you go out and start a family with some gold digging bitch. And that isn't even the deal breaker, you crushed my soul when you gave that trifling bitch something I tried over and over again to give you. A baby!" Rachel yelled.

She couldn't hold back the disappointment any longer. Reaching back as far as she could, she slapped Charles across his face and ran upstairs toward their bedroom.

Charles had no words for his actions so he decided to stay on the couch and let her calm down before they tackled the elephant that was in the room. All of his lies had been exposed and he didn't know how he was going to approach the situation. Nancy had struck again. He never thought this would happen. All of the secrets he was keeping from his wife was now out in the open.

# Chapter 7

Rachel awoke from her thoughts she had about Charles' infidelity that led to her decision that left a young girl and her mother dead. Charles had promised her he would never talk to or try to contact them again, but he had lied to her yet again. One day Rachel was thoroughly cleaning the house. She had her music playing and the whole house smelling like bleach and pine sol. While she was cleaning out Charles' office two weeks ago, she stumbled across the information he had hidden. There it was just lying there, a Baltimore address with the initials W and N written on it. It didn't take her to long to realize the initials stood for Winter and Nancy.

Rachel was heartbroken once again. Since he couldn't stay away from his other family for some odd fucking reason, Rachel took it upon herself to stop it. She had called her sister Madison's son, Greg who lived the street life in Baltimore. She knew it was wrong to ask him to do her dirty work for her, but something had to give. She couldn't keep competing with a side chick and a child.

After contacting him and talking to him about what it was she needed done, Greg ensured her his gang could handle it. Rachel had no remorse; no guilt clouded her mind. The hit was made. She went on about her business on a daily basis, with a smile on her face.

Back to reality Rachel drug herself out the bed and lit a Newport. She took two long drags and put the cigarette out on her plush white carpet. *I wonder how you take this news you fucking weak excuse of a husband,* Rachel thought to herself.

Rachel walked out her bedroom dressed in nothing but a long silk robe and black six-inch pumps. She headed to Charles office to drop the bomb he wasn't expecting. She sashayed in with her robe opened wide. Charles watched his wife walk seductively towards him, naked with a tight body. His dick jumped at the sight. He swiveled around in his office chair and let his wife seduce him with her eyes.

Rachel sat her juicy ass on Charles' desk and opened her legs wide revealing her perfectly shaved mound. A smile crossed her face before she smashed his face down in her swollen wet pussy. She let him make love to her with his tongue. She grinded her hips against the rhythm of his tongue. That was one of the things she loved about Charles, he was a pussy eating fool. He could suck her into ecstasy in a matter of minutes.

After twenty minutes of her gyrating her hips on his face, she reached her third climax long and hard all over him. It took her a minute to catch her breath. Only sound you could hear in the room was her panting. Once her heartbeat returned to normal, she slowly raised one foot and placed it in the middle of his chest, pushing him away from her. She turned around and arched her back so he could take her from behind.

Charles un-zipped his pants and let his twelve inches of hard, thick, mushroom-tipped dick, slide inside of his wife's pussy. The gushing sound told him she was wet as ever and it made him go hard with excitement. He pounded her all over his desk, pulled her hair hard, and pushed his shaft in her as far as it would go. Rachel screamed out in pleasure, as she backed her ass up every time the tip of his dick was just at the beginning of her pussy. They sexed for over an hour before they both exploded in unison.

"Whew! What was that for babe?" Charles asked as he pulled his clothes back on in a satisfying manner.

He flopped down in his seat trying not to pass out. He had sweat rolling down his face and back. He knew he had put in work.

"Because I love you," Rachel replied with a smile. She turned around to face him.

"Nawl that was more than just an 'I love you' fuck. What you up to?" Charles replied.

"Ok listen, I did something I know you wouldn't approve of but it was in the best interest for us. I want you to know even though what I am going to tell you is going to hurt, I need you to understand where I was coming from," Rachel responded as she stood up to close her robe and then sat back on his desk.

"What's wrong babe, talk to me?" Charles sat back in his chair.

"First off I'm going to keep this short and sweet. I cleaned your office two weeks ago, and what I found brought back former feelings of pain and betrayal. I found out that you have been still keeping tabs on that bitch and that bastard child of yours, when you promised me five years ago that you wouldn't. After feather thought I took it upon myself to handle the situation," Rachel told him.

"Handled the situation? Huh? What situation are you talking about?" Charles asked.

"Look, since you like taking matters in your own hands I decided to start doing the same," Rachel rambled.

"Woman, what are you getting at? You are talking in circles, get to your point." Charles knew he was caught again.

This wasn't supposed to have happened. He thought he had hidden their information in a safe place.

"Ok look, I had my nephew kill both of them and now as much as it hurts you but gives me satisfaction, your precious family is dead," Rachel said before she lit another square and blew the smoke in Charles face.

Charles just knew for sure his ears was playing tricks on him. *Did this bitch just say what I think she just said?* He thought to his self before he exploded.

"You did what? I know I didn't just hear you correctly!" Charles barked jumping out of his chair and quickly rushing Rachel, wrapping his large hands around her neck.

"You heard me BITCH! I said I had that family of yours killed!" Rachel screamed at him.

She was trying to fight him off but he was too strong for her.

"I can't fucking believe you Rachel! You had my daughter killed! My only child! And for what? For being born. You desperate, scorned bitch. She was my fucking daughter you slut." Charles hauled off and slapped Rachel across her face.

His hands was connecting every time they swung. He was livid.

"Fuck you nigga, she shouldn't have been born! What you expected me to do? Keep living this lie like she doesn't exist. Nawl fuck that, now she don't so whatever you want to do you better do it now cause after this, I'm leaving yo' bitch made ass for good," Rachel hissed.

She was now kicking and scratching at him. All of her anger was being released in that very moment.

Charles let Rachel's body hit the floor. He stood in the middle of his office stunned and grief stricken for his only child. He was always going to let her know about him but his wife took that decision from him, and all he could do was fall to the floor and cry out in pain. He cried from his soul. Now he couldn't make things right with Winter.

"How does it feel to know I now took something from you?" Rachel laughed picking herself up.

She stumbled to her feet and stood over him.

"Why Rachel? She was only a child. Why you do it?" Charles cried.

He didn't have any more fight in him.

"Now you hurt like I've hurt. Now you know how I feel. How does it feel to have something stripped away from you that you don't have any control over? I'm glad she is gone and now I'm out of here. I hope it was all worth it." With that said, Rachel stepped over her husband and walked back to her bedroom.

She made a detour to the bar to grab a bottle of wine off the rack and went up the stairs to her bathroom. She sat at her vanity and stared at her reflection in the mirror. She wiped away the tears that stained her face, straightened her posture, and smiled. She begin brushing her long curly hair, she had just had done not even two days ago. She stood and walked into her bathroom. She opened her medicine cabinet, grabbed her bottle of OxyContin, and the bottle of wine.

Emptying both bottles into her mouth, Rachel swallowed at least thirty pills of the poison. She kept pouring the wine down her throat and didn't miss a beat. She walked back to her bed and laid down, just waiting for the pills to take her away from this life. Forever away from Charles' cheating ass and away from her dead-end ass marriage.

# The Secrets He Kept

Charles on the other hand cried what seemed to be a river. He wanted to put a bullet in Rachel's head. How could she take something away from him that didn't belong to her? How could she betray him like that? He got up from the floor dusting off his pants and walked upstairs to his bedroom. He had to go find Rachel. He needed answers and needed them now. He just wanted to know why she would do such a horrible thing to his only child. His flesh and blood. He wanted to hold his wife and tell her he was angry with her but he also was still unconditionally in love with her.

Charles got to the top of the stairs and took a long deep breath before he opened up his bedroom door. He prepared his self for the worst argument they would have in their marriage. As he entered the room, he could see Rachel lying there quietly on her side of the bed with the covers pulled up over her shoulders.

"Rachel just tell me why her? Please," Charles asked grief stricken. "Rachel, I know I hurt you in the past but I haven't been with another woman since. What did my daughter ever do to you for you to have her killed? She was only eleven! She had a full life ahead of her now it's been taken away by you." Charles kept speaking to his wife without getting an answer and he was getting angrier by the minute.

"Answer me! Just answer me please," Charles hollered at his wife, this time with tears falling profusely.

Charles walked over closer to the bed and shook his wife hard but she didn't move. He pulled the covers back and shock took over his body, as he stared at his wife's lifeless body.

"No baby, no. You didn't have to do this! Just wake up for me baby, just please wake up," Charles said as he held his wife's body in his arms and rocked back and forth.

He searched for a pulse and held his head close to her mouth to see if she had a hint of breath still in her body. He laid her down on the floor and attempted CPR. He pinched her nose and held her head back, then began breathing air into the lungs of his beloved.

After five minutes of no activity from her end, he stopped trying, closed her eyes, and planted a kiss on her cheek. Charles got up and searched his room and bathroom to see what she used to take her own life. On the bathroom floor, he saw the empty OxyContin bottle and the wine bottle halfway gone. Charles went in his pocket to retrieve his cell and dialed 911 to report the death of his wife.

Charles sat on the floor next to his wife and thought about committing suicide his self. What did he have to live for? His wife was gone, his daughter was gone, and he didn't even have a pet to help him get over how he felt at that moment. His heart was being ripped out from his chest and he didn't have anyone to talk to about it. He watched as the ambulance lights got close up to his driveway, with police sirens blaring closely behind. Charles got up and left out to go let them in. Only thing he wanted to do was just give up, but he had a business to run and he wanted to go to Baltimore to go bury his daughter.

# Chapter 8

Winter was in CICU recovering from the last surgery to remove the bullets she still had in her. Still not out of the woods yet, she lay unconscious with heart monitors and breathing tubes inside of her body. Doctor Cole's heart hurt for the now little orphaned girl. He would stay well past his shift to take care of her and he ordered her a private nurse to take care of all her needs when he was too tired to do it. He knew it was against hospital policy to do the things he was doing, but he knew Greater Baltimore Medical Center needed his expertise. He was the best in his field and in a month's time, he was to be Chief Medical Officer.

The afternoon after Cherish Doe's surgery, Doctor Cole sat in her room after making his rounds to his other patients. He read to her out of his medical journals and some of his favorite books or magazines. In the few short days that she has been there, he had grown very fond of Cherish Doe. He checked in with the Baltimore Police Department often to see if she had any family members, but to no avail. They always told him they had no luck in contacting any more family to come care for her. He called CPS and they told him as well, no family asked about her and when or if she was better, they would come and get her. With no wife and kids of his own, Doctor Cole vowed to take care of Cherish Doe his self and show her someone was there to love her.

Doctor Cole would take her in and give her a life she never expected to have. If possible one day, he hoped she would allow him to he would adopt her. He checked her vitals once more before leaving to go have lunch with some colleagues. Doctor Cole stepped out of the room and went to the elevator to go to his office to retrieve his wallet and keys before he left the hospital, when he bumped into a small boy with a bunch of almost dead flowers in his hand.

"Hey young man," Doctor Cole called out to him but the little boy walked past Doctor Cole and paid him no attention.

"Do you need any help finding your mother?" he called out to the little boy again but didn't receive a reply.

Doctor Cole wanted to stop the little boy but he had business to take care of and he wanted to get back to getting Cherish Doe out of danger. He took a mental note to tell the nurses to watch Cherish's room just in case the people who tried to murder her came back to finish the job. He let the elevator close and prayed to God that Cherish would be alright until he got back.

After overhearing the nurse with the pretty, brown skin talk about a little girl they had no name on that was recovering from gunshot wounds, Abe just knew she was describing Winter. He listened intently so he could get a room number. It was amazing how they went on and not noticed him standing there all this time, soaking up the information they was unwillingly giving out. The nurse gave up the room number when she asked another nurse to go take a look at the Cherish Doe. Abe waited patiently for her to leave back out the room before he snuck in to see his friend.

Abe sat his fragile, bruised body next to Winter's bed and cried for the first time since the other night. He hated to see his only friend lying there halfway dead. He wanted to hold her hand and tell her how sorry he was for what he had done to her. About how he had let her down, he should have protected her. As Abe paced back and forth with his emotions running all over the place, he began to speak to Winter like she was standing next to him.

"I know you were right all along about the science homework. I didn't want to admit it at the time Winter, you was always smarter than me. So what's going to happen to us now? I fucked up Winter, I really fucked up this time. If I don't make this up to you I won't be able to live with myself." Abe walked closer to her and placed his hand on her heart. "I had to join Tristin's gang. I had no choice; he was going to kill me. In a moment of weakness I gave up on the best thing in my short life. After today I will never come see you again... just get better for me please." And with a kiss he placed on Winter's cheek, Abe walked out of her room, walking out her life forever.

Abe got to the elevator and pulled his jacket up closer to his face, and pressed the button to let the doors open. With a prayer he asked God to heal his friend and let her live a glamorous life without him. Without the pain of not having someone to take care of her and he asked God to bring someone into her life to love her as much as he did. The doors opened up and he got on, pressed the button for the lobby, and as the doors closed so did his heart. One day he was going to get back at his brother for having him do the un-thinkable; when he got older and stronger his brother was gone feel what he felt at that moment.

The elevator made it to the lobby and just as he was heading for the door, he ran back into the nosy Doctor that asked him did he need help finding his mother. When the two made eye contact, Doctor Cole saw so much hatred, guilt, and fear in the little boy's eyes he wanted to ask him did he need any help, but pushed the thought out his mind.

Abe saw how the doctor wanted to talk and rushed out the doors and ran for dear life.

Doctor Cole took out his phone and dialed the restaurant's number. Once the hostess answered, he informed her to let his colleagues know he couldn't make it today and that he would reschedule. He ran back to the elevator and pressed Cherish's floor. Doctor Cole was panicking. He pressed the button repeatedly like it would get there faster. Something just wasn't right with the little boy and something was telling him he knew Cherish. When the elevator reached her floor, he rushed out as fast as he could and ran into Cherish's room.

"Doctor Cole, is there something wrong?" Nurse Tammy asked him as he quickly rushed passed her.

"Get me hospital security, now!!" Doctor Cole screamed. He saw the half dead flowers as soon as he walked in the door.

He knew then that the boy had been there. He rushed to Cherish to make sure she was alright. He took her vitals and let out a long deep breath he had been holding on to since the elevator. He slumped down in a chair next to her bed when security came busting in her room.

"What's the problem Doc?" A heavy set security officer said to him.

"There was a little boy in here a few minutes ago. Find him now!" Doctor Cole yelled.

The security team rushed out of the room in search for the little boy.

"Aye you," Doctor Cole stopped one of the men.

"Yes sir."

"I want security on this little girl's room at all times, and if someone else comes to visit her, you let me know before you let them in," Doctor Cole ordered.

"Yes doctor, is there anything else you need us to do?"

"No, thanks for responding so quickly but when I leave here make sure you put your best man on the door."

The fat security guard left and went back to his regular rounds and Doctor Cole pulled his chair closer to her bed. He lowered his face in the palm of his hands; he couldn't understand why he was so protective over her. He didn't know her or her situation but his heart pulled him closer to her every day that she sat in that bed. When he held his head back up, he saw that Cherish had opened her big, wide eyes. He jumped up and pressed the nurse call button.

"What can I do for you Doctor?" Nurse Tammy walked in and asked him.

"Our patient has awakened and I need you here to help me take out her breathing and feeding tubes. She may want to know what's happened to her," Doctor Cole responded back.

Nurse Tammy worked quickly to help free Cherish from the machines that were once keeping her alive. When finally done, Winter looked from the doctor to the nurse and wondered where she was. Winter attempted to speak but her mouth was dry and the words would not come out.

"I know you are wondering what is happening to you but we will tackle that when we need to," Doctor Cole assured her.

Winter shook her head to signal to him she understood.

"My name is Doctor Cole. I was your surgeon. You came in here with four bullet wounds and you just recovered from your last surgery to remove the last two.

Now if you understand me shake your head," Doctor Cole instructed.

Winter shook her head once more but then signaled for Nurse Tammy to give her a drink of water. Doctor Cole gave the go ahead to do what she was told, and then she left out the room.

"I know all this must seem so surreal to you but just know I'm here to help you sort it all out. Just relax and get well. I will discuss some things with you, but just to warn you there will be some people, some detectives here to ask you some questions." Winter didn't know what this was all about but she hoped her mother got there quick to take her home because she was becoming frightened.

The nurse walked in with some ice chips and proceeded to rub them against Winter's lips, letting the liquid melt and sooth her dry throat. After Winter was finally able to speak, she signaled the Nurse that she was finished with the ice.

"Where is my mother?" Winter questioned no one in particular.

"We will discuss that when you are a little better honey, but for right now you have a wonderful team of doctors and nurses to help you," Doctor Cole said to Cherish as he placed a hand over hers.

Winter shook her head again and tears began to fall from her face.

"No need to cry darling, we have become so fond of you since you been here. We will give you some time to adjust but if you need anything, just press this button here and I or a nurse will be coming to your aid." With that being said, Doctor Cole and Tammy left Winter there with unexplained questions and a broken heart.

# The Secrets He Kept

All she could think about was if Abe knew she was in the hospital and that she needed him by her side. She turned her head to face the window and let the tears fall before she fell fast asleep.

# Chapter 9

Charles touched down in Baltimore soon as his wife funeral was over with. He was now on a mission, and that was to find his daughter so he could give her a proper burial. He was so grief stricken to the point his grief turned into anger. He had been to the city many times before this one so he knew his way around. He rented a car at the airport and was on his way. His first stop was to the Baltimore Police Department.

"Om excuse me, but I need to talk to someone about my daughter," Charles spoke to the officer.

"Give me a minute sir," the officer replied before turning her attention back to her computer screen.

The officer wasn't paying him any attention. She was in the middle of her game of solitaire and was about to win.

Charles stood in front of the desk waiting on the officer but he became impatient. "Excuse me ma'am, can you please get someone here to help me?" Charles raise his voice.

"How can I help you?" Detective Gonzales stepped in trying to defused the situation.

"Yes, I've been standing here trying to find out information about my daughter that has been killed. I just want to find out where this city keeps the bodies that haven't been claim," Charles huffed.

"Sir, how do you know the body hasn't been claimed?" Detective Gonzales questioned.

"I was told my daughter and her mother was killed together. I know for a fact they don't have any family here," Charles explained.

"Follow me," Detective Gonzales motioned.

They walked down the hallway to Detective Gonzales' office. He felt it was a more private matter and needed to be handle in privacy. Once inside his office, Detective Gonzales took a seat behind his desk and picked up his pen. He began his questioning.

"Ok, can you start by telling me your name?"

"My name is Charles Gates."

"Ok Charles, you mentioned something about you daughter being killed. Could you tell me all about it?" Detective Gonzales probed.

"They moved here about five years ago and I was just notified the other day that they were both killed," Charles said.

"Killed how?" Detective Gonzales asked.

"That I don't know of," Charles huffed.

He refused to become a snitch now. He only wanted the police to help him find Winter, not her killer. He had other plans for him.

"Who told you this?" Detective Gonzales jotted down some notes.

"My wife," Charles whispered.

"How did your wife come to obtain this information?" Detective Gonzales continued his questioning.

"Look sir, I don't know. She told me this and then killed herself. I just need to find my daughter," Charles argued.

He was becoming anger with the line of questioning.

# The Secrets He Kept

"Wait a minute, so you're telling me your wife told you, your child and her mother was killed and then turned around and killed herself?" Detective Gonzales was puzzled.

In all the years of being on the force, this was a first. The story screamed suspicion to the detective. He made a mental note to check Charles' story.

"Yes sir. I've been having a couple of bad days," Charles admitted.

"Ok, since you can't tell me that, can you tell me what your daughter's name is?" Detective Gonzales changed the subject.

"Winter. Winter Ann Gates," Charles stated.

Detective Gonzales wrote the name down. His heart went out to the torn up father who was only searching for his daughter. "Ok, give me a minute; let me have someone check our database." He walked out of his office leaving Charles with his thoughts.

Charles took a couple of deep breaths trying to relax his self. He felt like he was getting somewhere now. His mind was all over the place. Rachel killed herself and Winter was dead. His life was in shambles. He was brought out of his pity party by the sound of Detective Gonzales' voice.

"Ok, we have searched our database and didn't find anything to the nature of what you told me. The name Winter didn't show up at all. Is there anything else you can tell me? How was she killed?" Detective Gonzales pried.

"I don't know!" Charles yelled.

He was lost. He was for certain that the police would have something. Now he was empty handed.

"Well when you get more information, here is my card. Give me a call. Maybe I can help you then," Detective Gonzales told him.

# The Secrets He Kept

Charles couldn't believe his luck. He was being turned away by the police of all people. "Uh ok. Thanks for your help."

Charles walked out of the police station with nothing to go on. He hopped in his car; the next place would be the hospitals. He had to find her. He pulled out his list of hospitals in the area and the first one on his list was Greater Baltimore Medical Center. This was the hospital that was close to the last known address he had for them.

Charles walked in heading straight to the information desk. He waited in line until it was his turn. He had five people in front of him and by the looks of things, he would be standing there forever. He looked around the waiting room and he saw a couple holding a child in their arms. The child looked to be eleven years old, the same age as Winter. He could tell the child wasn't feeling well. He turned his head once he noticed the father looking at him like he was crazy. He watched as a man in a white jacket walked into a set of double doors.

Charles walked behind the man as quickly as he could. He made it behind the doors before they closed and locked him out. He began to read the signs on the walls. 'Morgue turn left' he read. He followed the signs until he got to the door with the word 'Morgue' in black letters. He pushed through the doors only to be stopped by another set of doors that were locked.

Charles rang the bell. He refused to turn around now.

"Yes, how can I help you?" a female voice came over the intercom.

"Yes, is there someone I can talk to about my missing daughter?" Charles spoke up.

"Sure, someone will be out soon," the woman said.

# The Secrets He Kept

Charles waited for someone to come help him. It took them another fifteen minutes or so to come assist him. After giving them the same description of Winter and looking through all of their Jane Doe's, he came up empty handed again. The hospital didn't have any kids that wasn't claimed. The woman also was helpful by calling three other hospitals in the area for him but got the same results. He thanked the woman and walked away.

*Damn it. I need to go holla at Madison. She can get in contact with Greg,* Charles thought to his self as he was getting into his car.

His stomach was growling and he was in need of something to eat.

# Chapter 10

"Doctor Cole, is this the little boy you were talking about?" The security guard announced as he walked into his office.

"Yeah, thanks for finding him for me," Doctor Cole replied coming from around his desk.

"Ok, what would you like for us to do with him?" the security guard asked.

"Leave him here. I would like a word with him for a minute," Doctor Cole told him.

"Yes sir," the security guard stated before turning on his heels and walking away.

"Ok don't go far. Depending on what this young man tells me, I might need for you to call the police," Doctor Cole said looking Abe in the eyes.

Abe heard the words police and instantly became scared. He didn't want them to call the police on him. He was halfway across the parking lot when the security guard caught up with him. He didn't know what to do so he just obeyed him and was brought back into the hospital. Had he known the police was going to be called on him he would have kept running. Now he was sitting in this office and was almost in tears. He didn't want the police to get involved because of what he had done to Winter. If they found out he would be taken to jail.

"No problem, I will be right outside the door," the security guard uttered.

Doctor Cole watched as the door closed before he started his questioning. "I passed you earlier on the elevator and noticed you held some flowers in your hands."

Abe nodded his head up and down.

"I asked you were you lost or needed help to find your mother, but you never answered me. What did you ever do with them flowers?" Doctor Cole probed.

"Om I-I don't know," Abe stuttered.

"C'mon now. You got to know what you did with them. Did you give them to someone special?" Doctor Cole bent down so he could be at eye level with him.

Abe just shook his head. He was scared.

"Ok, so who was that special someone?" Doctor Cole smiled.

"My friend," Abe smiled back.

The thought of Winter crossed his mind and it warmed his heart.

"Hey, I know your friend. I'm taking very good care of her. Can you tell me her name?" Doctor Cole pressed.

"Winter," Abe confessed.

"Ok, hold on one minute." Doctor Cole reached over his desk to retrieve something to write on. He was finally getting somewhere. He had her first name. Now it was time for him to get some more information. "Ok now, does Winter have a last name?"

"Duh, everybody has a last name," Abe smirked.

Doctor Cole laughed which made Abe laugh too. That lightened the mood.

"You are so right. Everybody do have a last name, like mine is Cole. What is Winter's last name?" Doctor Cole asked again.

"Gates. Her name is Winter Ann Gates. That's my best friend," Abe rambled happily.

"That's good, so how long have you two been friends?" Doctor Cole inquired.

"We've been friends for a long time. I love her. She is all I got. You going to make her better?" Abe started asking some questions of his own.

"Om, yes, I'm going to make her better but I need your help," Doctor Cole told him.

"Anything. I want to help you. What you need from me?" Abe bounced around in his seat.

"Tell me what school you guys go to?" Doctor Cole urged.

"Winand Elementary School. Our teacher name is Ms. Jenkins. Winter is smarter than me," Abe added.

"Oh I don't think so. You look like a pretty smart lil' fella," Doctor Cole joked.

"I am. I beat her every time in checkers. That's our favorite game," Abe bragged.

"Oh is it?"

"Yeah, we play it every time she comes over to my house," Abe replied.

"That sounds like fun."

"It is," Abe laughed.

"Does Winter have any family here?" Doctor Cole asked.

"No. She told me she may have a daddy but she didn't know where he was at and her mother..." Abe paused.

"What's wrong?" Doctor Cole pried.

"I don't want to get anyone in trouble," Abe admitted.

"Trust me no one will be in trouble. I just want to help her. Now I know this may be hard but I need you to answer me, ok?" Doctor Cole got serious.

"Ok," Abe agreed.

"Can you tell me how your friend got in here? What happened to her?" Doctor Cole inquired.

"I-I don't know." Abe shut down.

"C'mon now don't do that. I know you know what happen. Please tell me so I can help her. You do still want to help her right?" Doctor Cole probed. Abe shook his head. "Ok, that's good, so tell me what happened."

"It was a big fire. I tried to save her but I couldn't," Abe cried.

"You tried to save her how? Were you there too?" Doctor Cole muttered.

"I got there after the fire started. I had to save her. I hope she be ok. Can you save her now?" Abe cried harder.

Doctor Cole could see this was upsetting the little boy so he stopped. He handed Abe a tissue to clean his face. "Ok Abe, that's enough. You have helped me a lot. I thank you."

Abe cleared his face. He was happy the doctor told him he had helped him. That's all he wanted to do. "Can I go see her?"

"I don't think that would be a good idea right now. She needs her rest," Doctor Cole lied.

"When can I come back to see her then?" Abe asked.

"How about this, once she is better she will come see you. It's not safe for you to be around her," Doctor Cole scolded.

"Ok. Can I go now? I need to be getting home," Abe responded.

"It's getting late and you don't need to be walking home by yourself. Is there anybody I can call to come get you?" Doctor Cole questioned.

Abe's heart stopped. The only person that could or would come get him was his brother, Tristin. His only problem was Tristin would want to know why he was at the hospital. "Its ok, I only live two blocks up the street."

"Ok, how 'bout this, my shift is almost over so I will give you a lift," Doctor Cole suggested.

"Ok."

"Are you hungry?"

"Yes sir."

"Follow me." Doctor Cole led him out of his office.

He opened his door and told the security guard to take the boy to the cafeteria to get something to munch on and make sure he kept the boy in his sights.

Doctor Cole watched as the boy was led away. He was feeling hopeful for Winter now. Once Abe was out of his sight, he walked into Winter's room to do his last check of the night.

"Hello sunshine. How you feeling?" Doctor Cole praised walking up to her bed.

"Better," Winter whispered.

"That's good. I'm on my way out. I will be off for two days. You know how long that will be right?"

Winter acknowledged with a nod.

"Ok, here is my cell number, if you need anything just call me and I will come, ok?"

"Ok."

"The nurses will be here to help you and I got someone outside your door to make sure no one else tries to come here to hurt you. You are safe here."

"Ok. Have you called my mother? I really miss her."

"As a matter of fact, while I'm off I will try to find her for you," Doctor Cole lied to her.

"She lives at..." Winter told him her address and Doctor Cole wrote it down.

He says his good byes and left heading to go take Abe home.

# Chapter 11

It was Winter's last day in the hospital, and her emotions were all over the place from learning her mother had passed in the fire that night that almost took her life. After some time, they gave Winter a small box with her mother's ashes in them. Since no family came to claim her body, the hospital was forced to cremate her. Doctor Cole and Winter gave her a small, intimate funeral inside of Winter's hospital room just to pay her mother respect. She didn't know where she was headed in life and it was the scariest thought ever. The only thing that kept her sane was the father type relationship she had with Doctor Cole. He was beginning to be the only family she had in this world other than Abe, but he was nowhere to be found which broke her heart. She couldn't believe he abandoned her in her time of need and to top it all off, a social worker was on her way to take Winter and escort her into foster care.

Winter packed slowly, throwing the little items she had left in a hospital bag they provided for her, which was not much. Tears ran down her face and she fell back on the bed and cried some more. Her life couldn't be going in this direction; she had nowhere to call home her best friend and love of her life disappeared. Things just wasn't going to be the same anymore. Winter rose up out the bed, walked into the bathroom and washed her face. At that moment, Doctor Cole walked inside her room wearing a pressed white-collar shirt and tan slacks. He watched as Winter wiped the rag across her face. When she noticed him, the spark in her eyes finally came back and it put a smile on Doctor Cole's face. She ran and wrapped her arms around his waist.

"How are you feeling Winter?"

"Not so good Doc. The social worker is on her way to take me away. I don't know if I can survive in a foster home, I've heard so many bad things about those places."

He pulled Winter from his embrace and looked her square in the eyes.

"Winter, darling, you are stronger than you think... look what you just pulled through. I have faith in God that you will survive anything that comes your way from this point on." Doctor Cole gave her one last hug before the social worker, who Winter called Beth, walked in.

"Are you ready to go Winter?" Beth questioned.

"Yes ma'am," Winter responded.

Winter grabbed her bag off the bed and walked to the door with Beth, turned around and looked at the Doctor Cole, waved, and exited to her new life. He waved back to Winter and watched as she left.

Winter rode in the back seat of the car with Beth in silence, as she watched the hospital fade in the distance. She wondered did Doctor Cole miss her because she was going to miss all the attention she got from him. She never had a father in her life and she craved that father daughter relationship. As she looked out the window she vowed to never let anyone come back into her life just to leave her again. Heartbroken and confused, she looked forward to the future she was destined to have.

Thirty minutes later, they pulled up to the Children's Home, a foster home for kids. She looked at the four-story building and sighed. Kids were out front playing and adults rushed in and out of the building. It was a nice day out, the sun was shining and Winter's nerves were taking control of her body. Beth got out and opened the door for Winter to exit. She grabbed her belongings, held her head up high, and walked with Beth to the front door, to the beginning of the rest of her childhood life.

Winter has never been shy in her life, but being at that place made her feel out of place. She sat on the bed they appointed her, with her head hanging down twirling her plastic hospital bag in her hand. It was two other girls inside the room with her giggling to themselves. She tried to pay them no mind but they continued to giggle and point in her direction. Winter had enough of their monkey business so she decided to lie down. After meeting with the home director, Mrs. Colson for two hours and touring the grounds, she had enough for one day. She closed her eyes and shut her mind down from the outside world. The only thing she couldn't do was get Abe out of her mind and the thought of him somewhere playing and laughing with someone else other than her, had her all emotional again. Finally she pulled the thin cover they supplied her with up to her neck, and drifted off to sleep.

The next day, Winter woke up at eight to see that the other six girls that were assigned to the dorm, were already gone to breakfast. She hopped out of bed went to the bathroom to shower, get dressed, and head downstairs to the chow hall. As she walked in she looked around to see most of the kids eating and half playing around. She walked to the semi-full line and picked up a plastic tray, some dishes, and silverware to retrieve her food on. She walked behind a black girl with fiery red hair that she noticed was assigned to her room.

Winter wanted to run her hand through the girl's hair, that looked to be a little older than her. She had never seen anything so pretty in her life. It was like fire dancing on her head but not burning her. Not paying attention at the line moving so fast, she accidently bumped into her. Right then she thought it was going to be the first of many ass whoopings she knew she was going to receive.

"I'm sorry," Winter said with urgency.

The girl looked at Winter and smiled. "Oh it's no problem, and how are you doing? I'm Giselle Banks and you are?" Giselle asked as she placed her hand out so Winter could shake it.

Winter was so scared that she never looked the girl in the eyes.

"Darling, you don't have to be scared of me or this place. This is actually one of the good ones, what's your name?" Giselle questioned Winter.

Winter finally put her head up and spoke. "My name is Winter."

"Nice to meet you Winter," Giselle the red head girl said before turning back around, getting her food, and walking to the other side of the chow hall.

Winter's eyes never left the stunning girl and instantly she was drawn to her like a mosquito to a bloody arm. Winter placed her tray in front of the lady serving breakfast, got her food and walked in Giselle's direction. Winter didn't exactly know why she was following the girl but she had to at least try to make some friends in there, until that time came when she was sent away. She spotted her in a corner all by herself, so Winter took it upon herself to join the girl.

"Can I sit with you?" Winter asked.

Giselle looked up, scooted over, and patted the empty spot motioning for Winter to take a seat.

"How long have you been here?" Winter questioned trying to play the twenty question game.

"Over five months now," Giselle said while she dug into her food.

# The Secrets He Kept

"I just got here last night," Winter exclaimed.

Winter was nervous enough but she didn't want to pry into the girl's life too much, in case she didn't want to talk to her.

"I saw you when you came in you looked pretty tired, so I decided not to bother you," Giselle exclaimed.

She pushed her tray away from in front of her and stared at Winter with a loving smile. Winter didn't know how to react. She had one friend in her entire short life. For some reason she wanted to tell Giselle everything about her, in hopes she could make a new one.

"Well Winter, do you have your chore list, maybe we have some together, can I see it?"

Winter reached inside her only pair of faded jeans they supplied her with, and pulled out the sheet of paper the director gave her yesterday, handing it to Giselle.

Giselle accepted it opened it up and searched it intensely.

"Ok, here we go. We have chow hall duty later on today before they serve us lunch. I'll show you how to get it done in no time, just stick with me." Giselle handed Winter back her sheet of paper, grabbed her plate once more and continued to eat.

A smile graced Winter's face and she started to eat the bacon and eggs that sat in front of her. Five minutes later, a loud thud sounded off in front of Winter as she looked up at the butch girl that slammed her tray down on the table she sat at. Winter's smile had faded as she noticed she was one of the girls that giggled at her yesterday.

"Why are you at my table newbie?" the butch screamed at Winter.

She stood at least six feet tall to Winter, had pimples on her face, short black hair, and fat like a walrus.

"Leave her the hell alone Krystal," Giselle spat back.

"I will not Giselle, stay the fuck out my business!" Krystal screamed back, and sat across from them.

"She is my damn business and ain't nobody scared of yo' dyke ass."

"Yeah, we will see about that."

Giselle escorted Winter from the table, dumped their trays, and walked back off to their assigned dorm. As Winter walked up the stairs, tears fell from her eyes. She thought to herself, *How will I ever survive in here, I need my mother now more than ever.* When the girls got to the dorm, Winter didn't hesitate to run to her bed and let all the emotions she had built up, release out of her. Giselle sat by her side and gently patted her on the back.

"It's going to be ok Winter, she is more bark than bite. Do not let her frighten you, she thinks she runs this place."

Winter turned to face her new friend, wiped the tears with her shirt from her face and let out the biggest sigh.

"I'll be ok, thanks for everything, but you don't have to take up for me, I think I can handle myself."

"Have you ever been in a fight Winter?"

"No and I don't intend to," Winter stated.

"Well if you need me I'm here."

"Thanks Giselle."

Giselle walked to her bed and got ready to take a nap before chores began at twelve. Winter watched as her fiery red hair touched the pillow. She grabbed the covers and pulled them over her head and drifted off to some much needed sleep.

*"Please let me see my mom, I don't want to die,"* she cried as the assailant came towards her. He grabbed her by

her ponytail, dragged her into the front room and threw her on the couch. "Please! Just let my mom and me go, we won't say anything to the cops." The masked man put the gun up to Winter's face and let it trail down her chest and it rested by her navel. "Shhh, be quiet little bitch before I put a bullet in your pretty face."

Winter didn't resist anymore. All she could think about was not seeing her mom and Abe again. Her assailant tore her pants off her leaving her panties in place. "I wonder how you taste," he asked her. Winter squirmed at his touch and just when he was moving her panties to the side, she kicked him in the balls and ran for dear life, before he regained his balance and sent to shots to the back of her head. She didn't know why she didn't die at that moment but she wanted to. She laid in a pool of blood, her blood that leaked from her skull.

# Chapter 12

Tristin hadn't seen or heard from his brother in over a week. At first he didn't care what happened to him, but now he was worried about him. He and GMS would be going out looking for him today. They had gotten their money and didn't want Abe to start talking to the wrong people.

"Yo nigga!" Greg hollered through the phone.

"What's up fam?" Tristin replied.

"We need to talk now!" Greg yelled.

"Damn nigga, what the hell is wrong with you? Yo!" Tristin asked.

"Just get here man," Greg ended the call.

Tristin was a little taken back by the tone of his friend's voice. He busted a U-turn in the middle of the street and headed in his direction. He turned up his new mix-tape by Rich Homie Quan and hit the gas. Life was good for him now that he got his new car. He walked on the BMW car lot and brought a brand spanking new 2014 BMW X6. This was his dream car and after being paid from their last job and also keeping Abe's part of the money, he was able to walk away and still have a couple dollars in his pockets.

Tristin pulled up on Greg's street blaring his music out of his five twelves. He parked and hopped out, leaving the car running. To the local dope boys he looked like a God. Everybody on the block wanted to touch his new ride.

Greg watched his friend out the window. He just couldn't believe how careless Tristin was being. He liked the finer things in life too, but he knew not to go out and buy a brand new BMW without any income to prove how he could afford it. He raised his window to try to get Tristin's attention.

"Aye yo!!" Greg hollered.

Tristin waved him off and continued chatting it up with the youngins on the block. Greg watched as Tristin continue to talk for another ten minutes. He dapped them up and then handed one of them some money. He shook his head as he watched Tristin climb the three steps heading into his building.

Tristin walked into the house without even knocking on the door. "Aye man, what the hell was so important that I had to come here? Talk fast because I got some where to go."

"First of all, check yourself homie, I'm not one of them lil' knuckleheads you be dealing with that be riding your dick. Now my moms called and told me my aunt is dead," Greg stated.

"Say what?" Tristin was all ears now.

"That's what I'm talking about," Greg added.

"How? What happened?" Tristin asked.

"She killed herself," Greg told him.

"Killed herself? Damn that's fucked up. Did she leave a letter or something?" Tristin's mind was wandering now.

"Nawl I don't think so. My mom's ain't say nothing to me about it," Greg told him.

"So what that have to do with us? We should be free. She's dead," Tristin said smiling.

"Yeah, you right, but from what I hear her husband is also in town looking for his daughter. That nigga is crazy man," Greg muttered.

"Man fuck that nigga. He can get it too," Tristin yelled.

"Look man, I'm with that but I'm just concerned if my aunt told him it was us who took care of her problem," Greg sighed.

# The Secrets He Kept

"Man, get the fuck out of here with that shit. That's your people so you need to take care of this. I don't have a problem busting a cap in his ass too," Tristin snarled walking out the house.

He was done with the conversation. He hopped in his car and headed to find his brother. There were too many loose ends in the last mission. First it was Greg's aunt killing herself and now Abe was no were to be found.

Greg still felt uneasy about the situation. He knows the kind of man his uncle is. He now regretted not telling his aunt "no" when she called with the request. He broke the number one rule in the game and that was crossed his family. In his mind he had to get some more information on what Charles knew before he could make his move.

Greg locked up his spot and then set out to his mom's house to have a face-to-face talk with her. He had rushed her off the phone earlier because he didn't want to talk about the issue over the phone. His drive across town was a quiet one. He had some time to get his thoughts together before he pulled up in front of his mother's house.

Greg killed the engine on his 1999 Honda Accord. He watched his mother door for any signs of movement. Looking around his old neighborhood brought back memories of his childhood. He missed his old hood but vowed to never move back. Growing up for him, his mother always provided everything he needed but not everything he wanted.

Greg hopped out the car and headed to the door. He used his key to let his self in. "Ma!"

"What boy? Why you coming in here yelling?" Madison answered.

"I didn't know if you were here or not. I didn't see your car out front." Greg planted a kiss on his mother cheek as he always did.

"Yeah, my car been in the shop for a week now but your ass would have known that if you would call more," Madison told him as she walked away from him heading into the living room.

Greg already knew that was coming so he just kept his mouth closed and followed her.

"Sorry 'bout that ma, but you already know I be busy," Greg explained.

"Too busy? Chile please, it only takes you ten seconds to pick up the damn phone to call me," Madison replied.

"Ma I know and I will do better. So how you holding up?" Greg changed the subject.

"How do you think I'm holding up? I just found out my sister killed herself," Madison snapped.

"I'm still in shock. Auntie was a solider; I don't think she did that to herself. I can bet my last dollar that Charles had something to do with this," Greg piped.

"I don't think so. The police say it was an overdose. Enough about that. What brings you over this way today?" Madison piped.

"I came to check up on you and to see if you heard from Uncle Charles," Greg told her.

"No I haven't heard from Charles. The police was the ones to call me," Madison said.

"Did they say she left a letter or something?" Greg probed.

"No they didn't. Why are you asking all these questions like you really gave a damn," Madison huffed.

"Ma, I'm just trying to understand what is really going on," Greg lied.

*Ding dong*

They were interrupted by the doorbell.

"You expecting someone?" Greg asked.

"No, just go open the door," Madison uttered.

Greg got up and did as he was told. Opening the door he was face to face with a man he had never seen before. "How can I help you?"

"Om, looking for Madison, is she home?" Bret smiled.

He was a little taken back from the young man who opened the door.

"Yeah she here, come in man." Greg unlocked the screen door. "Ma you have company."

Bret followed Greg back into the living room. This was his first time meeting Madison's son. He had heard so much about him in the past.

"Hey bae. Thought you had to work today," Madison beamed as she wrapped her arms around his shoulders.

"I do in a few, but I just stopped by to check on you to see how you holding up," Bret murmured.

"I'm doing much better now that you are here," Madison cooed.

"That's good. Is there anything you need for me to do?" Bret asked as he took a seat beside her.

Greg stood in the doorway and watched their interaction. He still was unsure of who the man was and why his mom was calling him bae. He cleared his throat to make sure Madison knew he was still there.

"Oh I'm sorry Bret, but this is my son Greg. Greg, this is Doctor Bret Cole," Madison announced.

The two men shook hands as men do. "Nice to finally meet you. I've heard so much about you," Bret said.

"I can't say the same about you since my mother here hasn't mentioned you to me," Greg hissed.

"If your ass would come around more you would know what's going on in my life. I've been dating Bret for the last six months now," Madison explained.

"It's ok, I'm about to leave. I will call you once I go on my break," Bret blurted.

"No don't leave. My son was just about to leave. I need to talk with you about something," Madison hinted.

Greg was livid at the way his mother was acting. Without one word, he turned on his heels and walked out. He made a mental note to make sure he get on his mother at a later date.

# Chapter 13

Charles had been in the city for two weeks now and still had no leads on finding out anything on Winter. He had checked in with the Detective Gonzales twice. He started to feel like he was bothering him. The Days Inn had become his home for now. He had thoughts of returning back to Texas but had nothing there but business. He checked in with his right-hand man, Carlos to make sure his money was right, and to let him know he would be staying in Baltimore a little bit longer.

Charles finally had gotten the information he needed on finding Madison. He hoped she was home. He got dressed and headed for his rental. He had to make sure he renewed his rental as well. He headed to McDonalds to grab him something to eat and then headed in Madison's direction. On his drive over, thoughts of him killing Greg ran through his head. He was hoping Madison would tell him were he could find Greg but who was he kidding. No mother in the world would tell you where to find their child if you planned to harm them.

Charles' plan was to act as if he was going to question him to get the information on where he is at and then send him where Winter was. It was a must; Greg had to die for taking his only child's life. He shook the thoughts as his GPS signaled he was at his destination. He looked around at the many houses to make sure he was in the right spot. Looking down at the piece of paper he had wrote down Madison's address on, he was sure. He parked his car on the side of the road only because there wasn't any room in the driveway.

# The Secrets He Kept

Charles killed the engine on his car and then reached into the glove compartment to retrieve his .45. He could never be too safe. This wasn't his stomping grounds and anybody could get it at this point. He ensured he was straight before he hopped out the car. With slow but steady steps, Charles glided up the driveway. He stopped by the trashcan to get rid of the trash that was in his car. He walked up to the door and rang the doorbell.

Charles took a step back waiting for someone to come to the door. He could hear movement behind the door but didn't hear the locks open. He became suspicious. Taking two more steps back he removed his .45 and aimed it right at the front door. If the wrong person opened that door, he was going to empty his clip without the blink of an eye.

"Who is it?"

Charles heard a muffled voice speak. He refused to speak back. The front door had a peephole so he knew the person was looking right at him. He lowered his gun to his side out of eye shot. He leaned forward and rang the doorbell once again. He was now determined for the person behind the door to open it. Leaving wasn't an option for him. He was tired of all the dead ends he was getting in this state.

"I don't know who is at the door. They're not saying anything," Madison hollered right before she opened the door, only to be face to face with Charles' .45 aimed at her head. "What the hell?" She almost pissed on herself.

Doctor Cole rushed to the door once he heard Madison yelp out in fear. "Is everything ok?" he asked as he rounded the corner.

"Sorry Madison. I didn't know what was going to be on the other side of that door," Charles explained as he tucked his gun back in the waist of his pants.

"You scared the hell out of me," Madison held her chest. Her heart was beating a mile a minute. "Its ok honey. It's only my sister's husband," she turned to Doctor Cole and said.

"What are you doing here?" Madison turned her attention back to Charles.

"Do you mind if I come in for a minute so we can talk?" Charles asked not wanting to discuss his matter on the front porch.

"I kind of have company right now; can you come back a little later?" Madison stated.

"I'm only here for another couple of hours or so, then I will be heading back home. I just need to ask you a couple questions and then I will be out your hair. I promise I won't stay long," Charles lied.

Madison pondered what he had just said and unlocked her screen door against her better judgment. "Come on in. We can chat in the kitchen. Let me go let my boyfriend know what's going on." Madison led the way towards the kitchen.

Charles took it upon his self to take a seat. He could hear Madison and her male companion having a conversation. He could hear her explaining why she had to talk to him. He looked at his watch as if he had somewhere to be. Madison entered the kitchen as he was doing so.

"Sorry about that. How you holding up?" Madison questioned taking her a seat as well.

"My mind is all over the place right now. I tried to reach you about your sister's funeral. You know I loved your sister and to see with my own eyes her taking her life was heart breaking," Charles replied.

"So what really happened? The police called and told me she had taken her own life but that was it. They didn't go into details about why or how it happened, and I didn't have the money at the time to attend her funeral. Me and Rachel weren't even that close but I did and still do love my sister. So how did you go out?" Madison had a couple questions of her own to ask.

"Well, we had a big argument about something she found out and then it happened," Charles told her.

"Ok, but that's not really telling me nothing. What was you all arguing about?" Madison pressed.

"First I need to ask you something. Rachel told me some troubling news right before it happened."

Madison didn't even respond. She was waiting for him to tell her how it was, if he was with her sister was she able to kill herself without him trying to stop her.

"When was the last time you spoke with Greg?" Charles blurted.

"As a matter of fact, he was here earlier but I don't see what he has to do with this." Madison became defensive about her only child.

"He has everything to do with this. I need to talk to him ASAP." Charles raised his voice a little.

"Hold on now. I don't see how that can be possible if you live way across the damn state. Leave my son out of this," Madison yelled back.

"See, that's where you're wrong at. Before your stupid ass sister took her damn life she told me she hired Greg to kill my, my, my only child," Charles stuttered.

"Wait a god damn minute here, who the fuck are you calling stupid? Your pussy ass is sitting here telling me the reason my sister killed herself was because of an outside bastard child you had?" Madison hollered, bypassing the part about Greg being the one to kill his child.

"I'll show you a pussy. That bitch killed herself because she couldn't live with the fact she had Winter killed! She had better be glad she took herself out 'cause I would have," Charles huffed.

"Fuck you and that outside child Winter! You two bitches are the reason my sister is dead.

The argument between the two went from zero to one hundred quickly. Doctor Cole thought his ears were playing tricks on him. Had he just heard Winter's name being called? He got up from his place on the couch and moved closer toward the kitchen to get a better listen.

"Look, I don't believe what you are saying about Greg. He wouldn't hurt a child so Rachel lied to you. They didn't even talk," Madison defended her son.

"All I know is she said Greg was the one who killed Winter and her mother, so I need to talk to him to see what he has to say. I've been here in this damn state looking to claim my daughter's body and keep coming up short. I'm starting to think Greg did something with her body that's why the police can't find her," Charles explained a little nicer.

He could see that yelling at her wasn't getting him anywhere. He was now trying to trick her into telling him what it was he wanted to know.

"I don't know where Greg lives and don't have a number for him, but I'm telling you he did not do this." Madison stuck to her guns.

"So you really ain't going to tell me where he's at after I told you he is the reason my only child is dead?" Charles couldn't believe his ears.

"I can't tell you something I don't know, but if I did I still wouldn't tell you. You think I'm going to lead you to my boy, for what? So you can do harm to him? Not in this damn life time," Madison hissed.

Charles' trigger finger was itching and he knew he was at his breaking point. Madison left him no other choice in the matter.

"You can either help me find him so I can talk to him man to man, or if I have to go searching for him it ain't going to be nothing nice," Charles threatened.

He was done playing with her.

Doctor Cole had heard enough. He turned on his hells and walked back into the living room. Once he felt he had a good distance from the kitchen and he couldn't really hear them talking, he made his move.

"Baby! Can you come here for one minute?"

Madison didn't even excuse herself, she just got up at the sound of his voice and left Charles sitting there still talking to the back of her head.

"Yes love," Madison walked up on him, wrapping her arms around his neck.

She could feel his hesitation from her touch. She searched his eyes to see if anything was wrong. She hoped he didn't hear the conversation she had just had with Charles.

"I have to go. I just got a call from the hospital about one of my patients taking a turn for the worst. I will give you a call tonight once I get off," Doctor Cole lied.

He had to think quickly on his feet. He had to find an easy way to get out that house. He had heard enough about the reason Winter ended up in the situation she was in.

# The Secrets He Kept

"Awe bae, please don't go. I will get rid of him so we can finish what we started before he came over," Madison cooed running her tongue along the side of his neck.

"I would love to but I really have to go." With that he placed a kiss on her forehead and left with the quickness.

Madison couldn't believe what just happened. She stood in the middle of her living room floor confused. She forgot Charles was in the kitchen for a minute until he spoke from behind her.

"Can we please finish our conversation?"

"No, I think our conversation is over. You can see yourself out and don't come back. You no longer have ties with this family now that my sister is dead," Madison told him before disappearing down her hallway.

Charles didn't move an inch. He thought maybe she would come back out of her room but after waiting in the same spot for about five minutes, he gave up. He exited Madison's home with death on his mind. If she wasn't going to help him find Greg then he would do it on his own. For having to put so much work into finding him, Charles planned to just kill him just like he killed Winter.

# Chapter 14

Greg was chilling on the block when he noticed his cell kept ringing. Every time he looked at it, his mother's number would pop up. He was still pissed with her about the stunt she pulled earlier, so he ignored all of her calls.

Greg and Jon watch a group of fine ass women walk past them. He was in awe with their beauty. "Damn that bitch is fine," he dapped up Jon. "Aye baby, hold up a minute. Let me holla at you for a second."

He began walking towards the ladies and his phone went off again. Madison's number popped up and this time he opted to answer it. This was her ninth time calling him so he knew something had to be wrong. He answered the phone but didn't put it to his ear. "Aye baby give me a minute. I got to take this call. Jon, come 'ere man. Talk with the ladies why I handle this," Greg said pointing to his phone.

He took a couple steps away from the crowd before he placed the phone to his ear. "Yo."

"Boy I know you saw me calling you all damn day. Why haven't you answered my calls? Why the hell it took you so long to answer? I swear for God if I was standing by you I would slap the shit out of you," Madison ranted.

"Ma, calm your ass down. I've been busy today. What up though?" Greg sighed.

"There you go with that I've been busy shit again, but I bet your ass won't be so busy once Charles finds your dumb ass," Madison snapped.

"Hold up, what is you talking 'bout now?" Greg was all ears now.

"Charles is in town and looking for you," Madison screamed.

"Ma, how you know that?" Greg shrieked.

His heart rate picked up a bit. It seemed like everything with their last job is going wrong. Why was Charles looking for him?

"He came to my damn house making threats and shit. If your ass would have answered the phone earlier you would have known this," Madison uttered.

"What the fuck you mean he came over there making threats? Did that nigga hurt you?" Greg was livid.

In that moment he knew shit had gotten real.

"No, no he didn't hurt me. I'm just worried what he will do to you once he finds you." Madison had calmed down a little.

"Man, you don't have to worry about that. That nigga ain't gonna fuck with me. He has no reason to," Greg ensured her.

"Oh yes he does. Son, just be careful out there," Madison begged.

"Ma I am, but why would he have a reason to want to hurt me? I ain't did nothing to that nigga. Hell, I should be looking for him. That bitch ass nigga let my auntie kill herself," Greg babbled.

"Boy shut that shit up. It seems Rachel told him you were responsible for killing his daughter before she killed herself. Now he is out for bloo..." Madison couldn't even finish her sentence. The phone went dead.

Greg's whole world was flipped upside down. He couldn't believe his ears. Did he just hear his mother correctly? He had to find Tristin like yesterday. Forgetting about the ladies he had just stopped, Greg took off towards his car leaving Jon on the block. He peeled away from the curb driving reckless. He broke a coupe laws by running red lights and stop signs. He was also pushing his little car to the max.

Greg was trying to keep his eyes on the road while he kept pressing end on his cell. Madison was back to blowing up his phone. He couldn't take it anymore. He turned his phone off and threw it in his passenger seat. He had no time to talk to his mom. This was a life or death situation that needed his undivided attention.

Greg whipped his car in front of Tristin's front door. He hopped out leaving the keys in the ignition. He didn't care if someone stole his car. That was the least of his worries. He had a killer after him and had to warn his boys. He began banging on the door like his life depended on it. His knocks went unanswered.

Greg made a dash for his car. He retrieved his cell phone powering it back on. He waited until his home screen popped up and then searched for Tristin's number. He found it and pressed send. He tapped his feet waiting for an answer. The phone stopped ringing which meant Tristin answered it. "Aye yo, where the fuck you at?"

"I'm out looking for my lil brother. I haven't seen that nigga since that night. What's good?" Tristian asked.

"How far are you from your crib?" Greg piped.

"I'm over here on the West side by the hospital," Tristin replied maneuvering in traffic.

"So you over by my mom's house?" Greg uttered.

"Yeah, you can say that. Man, what's going on?" Tristin probed.

He was now on alert. Something just wasn't right with his right-hand man.

"Aye just swing by my mom's crib and I will be pulling up in 'bout ten minutes. We need to talk. Hell, I think its best you hear this shit from the horse's mouth anyways." Greg was walking and talking.

"Folk, you talking in riddles, man. What's really going on?" Tristian made a U-turn heading in the opposite direction.

"I got you once we get to my mom's crib." Greg ended the call.

Nothing else needed to be said. He hit seventy up the street. The fifteen minute drive only took him eight minutes to get to his mother's side of town. He bent a left by the hospital and thought his eyes were playing tricks on him. ABE!

Greg spotted him walking through the hospital parking lot. He swerved over almost causing a wreck. He swooped into the parking lot, but by the time he brought his car to a complete stop, Abe was walking through the hospital doors.

Greg slammed on his breaks and ran through the doors also. He looked around wildly until he caught the back of Abe's shirt walking on the elevator. "Abe!"

Abe turned around to see a familiar face coming towards him. He was terrified. He thought for sure Tristin had sent the goons to find and kill him. He crouched down in the back of the elevator unable to go anywhere.

"Yo Abe! Come here. Your brother is looking for you." Greg ran towards the elevators.

He ran to catch the elevator but was three steps too late. The door closed before he could get there. "Fuck!"

Greg pressed the button repeatedly willing it to come back down with Abe still on it. People in the hospital began to look at the way he was acting. He looked around and saw the stares and decided to just leave. He will get Abe another time. He walked out the hospital with some pep in his step. Hopping into his car he drove towards his mother's house.

Greg pulled up in his mother's driveway and noticed Tristin was still sitting in his car. He killed the engine on his car and jumped out. He signaled for Tristin to follow him and continued towards the door. He rang Madison's doorbell five times. He didn't have time to reach for his keys.

"How 'bout I just saw your brother heading into the hospital," Greg announced, as Tristin got closer to him.

"Yo why you didn't grab that lil' nigga?" Tristian huffed.

"Nigga I tried to but his ass is fast. He had just gotten on the elevator by the time I caught up with him," Greg laughed.

Before Tristin could respond, the front door flew open and Madison walked out the house swinging. She slapped Greg upside the head three times before she said one word.

"What the fuck I tell you about hanging up that phone on me?" Madison yelled.

"Ma chill! Damn." Greg tried to block the blows but he wasn't quick enough.

"Get your ungrateful ass in here before I fuck you up," Madison barked and turned on her heels still talking shit. "Stupid motherfucker, I was trying to tell you something to save your motherfucking life."

"Damn your momma is an OG." Tristin laughed at the way Greg just gotten beat up.

He had heard stories about how Madison got down but to see it for his self it was amazing.

"Lock my motherfucking door!" Madison hollered.

Greg and Tristin both followed Madison while she was on her rampage, neither saying one word, both scared to interrupt her.

"Sit y'all ass down and tell me what the hell y'all been doing in them streets to have niggas coming to my motherfucking house," Madison demanded.

Tristin gave Greg a crazy look like 'What she talking about?' Madison caught the look and took off on them again.

"Oh, so you ain't tell your boy what's going on?" Madison stated.

"Ma we been chilling. We ain't did shit," Tristin spoke up.

"You lying!! Greg open your damn mouth," Madison told him.

"Ma Tristin telling you the truth. We ain't been doing shit but chilling," Greg lied.

"So what y'all telling me is that what Charles said y'all did to his lil' girl was a lie?" Madison said with clench teeth.

Tristin shot Greg a look of horror. He was shocked anybody had knowledge of that night. He jumped up as if his seat was hot. He was now feeling like Greg. The boys both knew this was a serious situation.

"Ma, what did Charles say exactly and don't leave out nothing," Greg whispered.

Madison told them about the conversation she had with Charles from start to finish. By the time she got to the end, both of their mouths were hanging open. They now had too many loose ends that needed to be clipped.

"Damn," was all Tristin could say.

"We got to handle this nigga as soon as possible. I know him man and he is out for blood. This nigga is a straight killer," Greg explained to Tristin. "Ma is that all he said to you?"

"Yeah, my boyfriend was still here and he left because Charles was getting loud as hell in here," Madison revealed.

"Fuck!" Greg yelled and walked out the house with Tristin on his tail. They not only had to find out where Charles was at, but now they had to find out how much did Doctor Cole knew about the situation. This was beginning to be a mess they couldn't afford to let slip pass them.

# Chapter 15

Detective Gonzales sat at his desk that bright Saturday afternoon, going over a cold case he had been trying to solve since last December. Usually his conviction rate was high but now it seemed like he couldn't get past go with his open cases. Now here it is he had two open cases with no leads to follow and it was starting to bug the hell out of him. He leaned back in his chair and scratched his head then threw the file back on his desk. He grabbed the Jane Doe file and walked into the squad room, heading over to the coffee pot to pour him a cup of Joe. He filled his paper cup almost to the rim with the hot liquid, since he only drank black coffee. He blew at the top to warm it some before he drunk it. It wasn't the best coffee in the world, hell it wasn't even the best coffee in the building, but he drunk it nonetheless.

Detective Gonzales leaned up against the wall in the squad room then opened the Jane Doe file. He took a look at it once again just in case he missed something. As he looked at the crime scene photos of the twelve-year-old girl that survived that horrible night he thought to his self, *Who in their right mind would try to kill such a beautiful young girl even though they didn't succeeded? With her mother, yeah, why her though, did she see their faces? Was this a drug deal gone badly or was this a crime of passion?*

Question after question ran through his mind. After thumbing through the rest of the pictures one thing was for sure, he would not get a lead from looking at the pictures of her mother after the fire had consumed her whole body. All that was left of her was ashes and some teeth. The medical examiner determined that it was a homicide. At least nine bullet casings where found at the scene. The fire marshal declared that the fire was set by using a flammable liquid, like lighter fluid to engulf the house in flames. All he needed now was the caller who phoned in the incident and the names of the victims, as he waited for the DNA results to come back. Once the DNA results came back, hopefully the unidentified woman's name was in the system.

Still going over the file, Detective Gonzales' phone on his desk started to ring. He hoped it was the medical examiner with good news. He raced to the phone to pick it up after the fourth ring.

"Gonzales," he spoke into the receiver.

"Yo Gonzales, how's it hanging man?" the medical examiner piped.

"I'm good Peter; tell me you got some good news for me?" Detective Gonzales huffed.

Peter Castiano, the Baltimore medical examiner sighed through the phone.

"I'm sorry to let you know this but I couldn't ID the woman. Her dental records are not on file and since we have no picture of how she looked, I can't run her face in the database and to top it all off, there is no visible DNA to match it with," Peter blurted.

"I knew this shit was going to be all bad. Thanks anyway man. When you get off drink on me?" Detective Gonzales asked.

"I'm with that and I don't want the cheap stuff you like either," Peter laughed into the phone.

"I got you man, let me get back with you later on today." Gonzales hung up the phone and plopped down into his seat.

He opened his desk drawer on the right hand side and threw yet another cold case file on top of the other cases he had yet to solve. Two things were for certain; he needed DNA from the victim's daughter and he needed to go over the 911 tape again. He exited his desk and walked over to the file cabinet that held the other evidence of the case.

Detective Gonzales searched for the 911 tape of Jane Doe, the pulled out the tape and recorder. He pressed play and listened intently at everything that was wrong or right about it. He played close attention to the background noises and the way the caller's breathing sounded when he let the operator know what was going on. He heard a kid's voice. The child couldn't be any older than the victim's daughter. In his gut he knew that they had to know each other.

Detective Gonzales pressed stop after it finished then pressed play one more time just to make sure he didn't miss anything. *This shit is getting frustrating, how can a little boy pull her to safety just to leave her there to fight for herself. They had to have known each other. Where are you, you little fucker, I need your help,* Gonzales thought to his self. He grabbed up the evidence, walked back up to his desk and prepared to leave. This case was getting the best of him and all the hours he has put into it was starting to affect his way of thinking.

Detective Gonzales grabbed his gun and put it back in his holster, put his badge on the waist of his pants, took his jacket off the back of the chair, and placed it on his left shoulder. Everything he needed to take home to try to solve this case was in a cardboard box in his arms.

As Detective Gonzales walked away from his desk, his phone started to ring and since he was ending his day he let it ring. He got his right foot outside of the door as soon as the voicemail picked up, and out came a message that was going to change the course of events from here on out.

"Hi Detective Gonzales, this is Bret Cole speaking, oh excuse me, this is Dr. Bret Cole speaking. I have some information that I need to talk to you and only you about. Can you please give me a call at..."

Before he could even get the number out, Gonzales dropped everything in his hands and rushed to the phone to pick it up. Yes, finally, he was getting somewhere with this case maybe this information was just what he needed to break it wide open. He reached for the phone and hurriedly talked before he hung up.

"Yes, yes Doctor Cole, I'm here. What information do you need to give me?" he asked out of breath.

"Are you in a rush sir, 'cause we need to talk privately about what I have to tell you." Doctor Cole was relieved he answered.

This had been weighing heavily on his mind.

"No, I'm in no rush and let me go into an empty room so we can have some privacy. Can you take down my cell number and call me back?" Detective Gonzales uttered.

"Sure, what is it?" Doctor Cole asked while he searched his car for a piece of paper and pen.

"Its 555-2367."

"Thanks, give me a few seconds and I will call you back." Cole hung up the phone and let a few minutes pass to let Gonzales get settled in the private room. He searched aimlessly around the car for nothing in particular. He didn't know if he was doing the right thing by divulging this information, but being as though he thought he was Winter's protector, he had to at least try to get someone other than a twelve-year-old boy on his team.

Doctor Cole gave Detective Gonzales five more minutes before he called him back. He dreaded this call but knew it had to be made. He dialed the number and hoped to

God the decision he was about to make didn't put Winter in any more jeopardy than she already was.

"Look, I don't have much time, so I'm just gone tell you everything I know," Cole spat into the phone when Gonzales picked it up.

"I'm settled in and you have my undivided attention," Gonzales retorted back.

"Well I have been dealing with this lady for six months now, and today out of all days when I go over to spend some time with her, her brother-in-law comes over pointing a gun at her. She soothed him down to the best of her abilities. Now to make this long story short, after the incident they go in the kitchen and have a heated conversation about his infidelities and her sister killing herself about them," Doctor Cole babbled.

"Hold on, wait a minute, what does this have to do with my case? I don't have a suicide I'm working on," Detective Gonzales snapped, it never dawned on him that the man that came into the station was the same man Dr. Cole was speaking about.

"I know but this is where things get interesting. My instincts told me to leave but what caught my attention to stay was what I heard next." Gonzales sat there listening to the story wishing he would just get to the point of his call. "I overheard him say he was just here to bury his daughter and her mother. Now I didn't know what the fuck was going on so I was leaving since the argument turned into just a plain conversation."

"Ok Doctor Cole, is that what this call is about, a deceased woman and her child?" Detective Gonzales tried to clarify.

Doctor Cole sighed, and frustration was evident on his face so he just kept going on with his story.

"Look, I know I'm rambling but you just have to listen to everything. They said Winter's name and her mother's name is Nancy, and that she left years ago to get away from him," Doctor Cole finalized.

"Who is Winter and Nancy?" Gonzales questioned.

"Winter is the Jane Doe that was found shot outside of the burning house and Nancy is her mother whose remains are in your morgue. Winter is alive and well. She is living in a foster home under Jane Doe. I have been protecting her since she left the hospital after she got better."

"So you're telling me that the victims of the double homicide I have been working on is the same one's they were discussing?" Detective Gonzales couldn't believe his ears.

"Yes detective, that's what I'm saying. I don't know the whole story because I was eavesdropping, but I am positive that her son and his friends had something to do with the mother's murder and the shooting of Winter. I am no longer at her house but sitting in my car a few miles down the road."

"Look, I am about to leave, can you meet me somewhere we could talk more about this?" Gonzales asked.

"Yeah, can you meet me at Susie's Bar and Grill in downtown in an hour?" Doctor Cole checked his watch.

"I'll be there in forty-five minutes," Detective Gonzales declared.

The phone hung up and Detective Gonzales ran out the station. He got into his Dodge Ram and headed towards the downtown area. Things were starting to look up thanks to that call.

# The Secrets He Kept

# Chapter 16

Charles didn't know why he followed the man that had just left Madison's house. He just knew something was off about him and how abruptly he left following the conversation he had with Madison. He watched as he sat up the road from her house, intently talking on the phone. Against his better judgement, he followed him anyway when he pulled off going towards the downtown area of B-more. Even when he should be looking around for Greg, something told him in his gut that he was on the right track.

****

Gonzales made it to the meeting spot in less than an hour. As promised, as he sat in his car waiting on the doc to arrive, he flamed up a Marlboro cigarette, inhaled the smoke, and let it pass out his nose. Smoking always soothed his nerves. His ex-wife hated that he smoked and that was one of the reasons why he divorced her crazy, cheating ass. He pulled three times off the cancer stick and snubbed it out in his ashtray. Moments later a Benz pulled up in the lot of the dining establishment. Guessing it was the doc, he stepped out and waited by his car while he found a park.

Doctor Cole parked his car a few feet away from the entrance and walked over to where the detective was standing. When he got close to his personal space, he extended his hand to give him a handshake. Gonzales accepted it with no problems. Once they got the pleasantries out the way, they got straight down to business.

"Do you want to go inside and talk?" Cole asked.

Meanwhile, Charles pulled in behind Doctor Cole. He parked a few cars down from the two men with his window halfway down. He listened intently at the conversation the two was having. By the looks of things, the conversation was about to get deep. He picked up his cell acting like he wasn't paying attention to them and tuned in to their conversation.

"No, no, I don't want the risk of anyone hearing our conversation, we could just talk here if you don't mind," Gonzales responded back.

"Well like I said, Winter is very much alive."

"How did you even know her name to even know who those people where referring to?"

"Well, she had a visitor in the hospital, a little boy by the name of Abraham. He told me everything that happened that night and how if the people that finds out she is still alive, they will come and try to kill her again."

"Do you have a number on this boy Abraham?" Gonzales said, while all the time he was deriving a conclusion, thinking this boy was his 911 caller.

"No, he calls me from time to time and I don't know his whereabouts either before you ask."

"So this Charles character, you think he wants her dead?"

"I don't know what to think at this moment. He was saying he was her father. All I want to do is keep Winter safe, that's it, that's all."

"I understand how you feel Doc. This case has gotten personal to me too. If you want, we both can keep her safe until I find the bastards that did this to this family."

"I will be adopting Winter sometime soon, Detective, and I want this part of her life to be behind her," Doctor Cole announced.

"Ok, can you give me the rest of the names that you heard were involved and the description of this Charles character? I want to run his name."

# The Secrets He Kept

"I didn't get too much info from the conversation. All I heard was Charles was looking for Greg because he murdered them. Now if you are going to help Abe and me out with keeping Winter alive you must know where she is at." Doctor Cole explained.

Charles listened to what was being said and couldn't believe his ears when he heard his name and Winter's name, but when the Doc got to the part of revealing where Winter was at, it was almost as his voice went into a whisper.

*Damn!* Charles was frustrated. He knew that Doctor Cole was acting funny and was glad that he followed him. And now he was talking to the same detective that wouldn't give him any help earlier when he got into town.

*What the fuck is going on around here and why is this man meeting with a detective soon as I go talk to Madison? I see I'm going have to dead both these niggas. I don't care if one of them is a cop. After I find my daughter, I'm getting the fuck out of B-more and back home,* Charles thought to his self.

Gonzales noticed a suspicious car with a man just sitting there but couldn't see his face. He let his paranoia go and chopped it up as the man waiting for his date to arrive. After Doctor Cole informed him where Winter was, they talked a little more, then both of them went their separate ways. Doctor Cole had to get to the hospital and pull a double and Gonzales had to get home to make some sense of what the fuck the two victims in his case ever did, to make someone viciously attack them, as he made his way back to his car and pulled off.

Detective Gonzales rode from downtown on his way home, thinking of everything Doctor Cole had told him.

*"Now that I remember her last name is Johnson so I'm thinking her son name is that also."* Cole confessed to him.

*"And this Charles fellow, what is his?"*

*"I'm assuming its Gates since Abe told me that's Winter last name, but I can't tell you any more than that."*

*"It's ok Doc, thanks for what you did and thanks for what you're doing for that little girl. She needs someone in her corner right now."*

Detective Gonzales shook his head to get out the reverie he was in since he has gotten the information. His police juices were flowing. First thing tomorrow morning he was going to look into Greg and his known associates, put out an APB on their whereabouts, and go from there. He had a slight headache from all the new information he just learned. He pulled up into a gas station to grab some aspirin, when he noticed the same car that was parked in the lot speed past him.

Detective Gonzales thought nothing else of it. He walked into the gas station, and paid for some Bayer aspirin that was way too damn high for his taste, but he needed them. He walked out and swallowed the pills without a drop of water to let them go down smoother.

After leaving the gas station, the ride home was a pleasant one. He turned on a smooth jazz station on his radio and let the sounds of the sax and trumpets take him into another world.

****

Charles knew he couldn't get to the Doc because he heard him saying he was going to be at work and he couldn't afford for people to see him put his death game down. He would have to wait until the next time. So he chose to follow the detective to his home since he overheard that was where he was going. For a minute there, he thought he was spotted so when he turned into the gas station to do whatever he went in there for, Charles sped up and rode past him so he wouldn't be thinking he was following him.

After an hour drive, they were finally at their destination. Charles slowed down to an almost complete stop and watched the detective go inside of his small but nice house located in a decent neighborhood. He was glad it was kind of late and dark out. No one was around to witness what he planned to do in less time it would take for him to tie his shoe. He parked his car at the corner of the block and walked to the house directly in front of the detective's to watch his every move.

Charles sat and watched from the bushes, at how he maneuvered around in the house. He checked his watch and it said a little past midnight. He was getting antsy waiting for the detective to settle down so he could make his move. When the front room lights went out and the only thing you could see was the glare from the TV, Charles made his move across the street to get a better view of his target. He poked his head into the sheer curtains that graced the window and watched how the detective chugged on a beer and watched ESPN. That was his cue to go through the back door.

Charles walked around to the back making sure didn't any neighbors see him entering the yard. He approached the back door and let his breaking and entering skills come back to life one more time. He was once a burglar in his youth, but that quickly got old when he started to make real money dealing drugs. After playing with the lock for a good four minutes, he was finally in, making sure to leave the door open so he wouldn't be detected if it squeaked or it slammed closed before he got to make his move.

# The Secrets He Kept

Gonzales never saw Charles coming but he did hear the hammer being cocked on the gun that was now raised to his head.

"Whoever you are, you do know I'm an Officer of the law?" Gonzales spoke.

Charles came around to face the detective but kept the gun trained at his head.

"Do you remember me Detective Gonzales?" Charles questioned.

Gonzales put his beer down on the table to the left of him and cleared his throat.

"Yeah I remember you; you came in the station asking about your deceased daughter. Now since that's out the way, why are you in my home?" Gonzales said while he smirked at Charles.

Charles being the ruthless drug dealer that he was didn't find anything funny in the corny ass joke the detective made, so he turned the gun around and slapped him hard as hell in the mouth.

*Ahhh!* Gonzales screamed!

"That will teach you to stop cracking dumb ass jokes while you're in the interrogation room," Charles said making a joke of his own.

"I'm going to put you under the jail for that playa," Detective Gonzales replied spitting out blood.

"Nigga after this and only after you give me the information that I need, I promise you your death will be quick," Charles threatened.

Gonzales spat blood on the floor next to Charles' feet, signaling he didn't give a fuck.

"You disrespectful motherfucker!"

Gonzales laughed and picked back up his beer and took a sip. He wasn't fearing Charles at all. It was funny how a man can come to another man's home with such disrespect and think he was going to get anywhere.

"Where is my daughter and her mother so I can bury them?"

"Give me their names so I could find out."

Charles smacked him again across his mouth with the gun.

"Stop fucking beating around the bush. I heard you talking to that man, now just tell me where they are at!"

"I can't do that sir, so either you gone have to kill me and find them on your own or let me go and hope you can find them when you get out of jail."

Charles was getting pissed. Now his anger was evident on his face and Detective Gonzales just sat there smiling from ear to ear still sipping on that Old Style beer.

"So I see you don't want to help me out. Suit yourself."

Charles emptied his clip inside of Detective Gonzales' chest. Thank God he decided to put a silencer on it because the sound would have woke the hood up. Smoke came from tiny holes in the detective's body and his beer still sat in his hand. Charles left out with no information and it was back to the drawing board for him in locating Winter. Now he was off to handle Greg; he'll have a conversation with the doc later.

# Chapter 17

Weeks had passed since Winter had been in the Children's Home. She and Giselle had become real good friends, especially since she kept Krystal off her ass. Krystal tried her best to get Winter alone to do harm to her; she couldn't understand why she hated her so much. She asked Giselle plenty times why she tried to harm her but all she told her was if you don't love yourself how could you began to love something else. Winter pondered what Giselle had said and she was right.

Winter was in the chow hall cleaning up after lunch by herself. Giselle had to go see her case worker so she was left alone in the kitchen washing dishes for dinner. As she scrubbed and rinsed each dish, she noticed that Krystal was coming inside with a devilish grin on her face. She walked into the kitchen and stared at Winter. She tried not to pay Krystal any mind but the stare alone was burning a hole in Winter's neck.

"I knew one of these days I would get you by yourself," Krystal said while she locked the kitchen door and walked up to Winter, then ran her fingers through Winter's hair.

"The, they will be back," Winter stuttered.

"Yeah they will be, but not before I get to play with you."

Krystal turned Winter around and pushed her against the sink. She tried to fight her off but she was much stronger than she was. As they both struggled, Winter finally got a hand up and pushed Krystal away, but it didn't do much because she was right on her. She punched Winter in the face so hard it felt like her jaw broke and she fell face first to the floor. Krystal kicked her several times in the stomach before Winter balled up to block some of the blows. She then bent down to rip off Winter's pants then grabbed a mop and broke it in half.

"Let's have a little fun," Krystal said as she bent down and ripped Winter's panties off and shoved the mop handle inside Winter's virgin pussy. *"Ahhhh!"* Winter screamed as the tip penetrated her insides. Krystal savagely abused her repeatedly. When she wasn't ramming the mop handle inside of her, she was beating her across the back with the other half.

It felt like hours had passed before Krystal had stopped and left Winter bleeding on the kitchen floor, but it was only minutes. Winter scurried under the steel counter and cried until a counselor found her bleeding profusely on the floor. The counselor tried reaching out to Winter but she sat there terrified and shaking. Giselle came in moments later, threw her hands to her mouth and gasped at the sight that was in front of her. She bent down not bothered by the blood she sat in, and went to Winter's aid. When Winter finally saw that it was Giselle that was by her side, she instantly moved closer to her and whispered in her ear.

"I have to get out of here Giselle," Winter cried.

"Tell me who did this to you Winter?" she asked lovingly.

Winter just shook her head and said nothing. The counselor finally walked to the phone to call an ambulance to get Winter the help she needed.

The two friends stayed side by side until the ambulance arrived and escorted Winter to the hospital. By then the entire Children's Home was outside looking around, saying their ooh's and ahh's. The only person that didn't look concerned was Krystal, who had the ugliest smirk on her face. She turned around when the ambulance pulled off and walked into her dorm room, with Giselle fast on her tail.

Giselle slammed the door behind her and got into Krystal's face.

"I know it was you, who did this to Winter!" Giselle screamed while she poked her finger in Krystal's face.

Krystal stood tall in Giselle's face and smacked her hand out her face.

"You don't know shit and if you don't want what happened to that scary little bitch to happen to you, you will stay out my face," Krystal threatened.

"I don't know what the fuck you think this is but I'm not one of these little girls in here who are scared of you. One of these days all the wrong shit you dish out will come back to bite you in the ass. You do know karma is a bitch and I can't wait until she finds and murders yo' sadistic ass."

Giselle turned and walked towards the door to go find out what hospital they had taken her friend to. She felt she needed to protect her. She was steaming mad she wasn't there to help Winter when she needed her. But before she could completely get out the door, Krystal grabbed her by her ponytail and punched her in the head. Giselle felt the stinging blow but it didn't faze her. She instantly got out of Krystal's grasp and punched her straight in the face making Krystal back up some. Krystal shook the punch off and charged back at Giselle. Blow after blow each girl sent landed. They wrestled, kicked, punched, and bit each other.

Giselle landed on top of Krystal and landed punch after punch to her face. She had so much anger and rage coming out of her. It sent her into the thoughts of why she was there in the first place then the tears started to roll. The commotion was so loud that the director and some counselors came running up the stairs to break up the fight. They grabbed each girl off each other.

"Let me go, she was the one who did this to Winter. I just know it's her!" Giselle stated.

"You don't know shit!" Krystal screamed.

The director looked at each girl. When she saw the truth in Giselle's eyes she knew she wasn't lying. She snatched up Krystal and escorted her to her office.

"I'm gone fuck you up Giselle!" Krystal hollered going down the stairs.

"You can try dyke bitch!" Giselle yelled back.

Once the counselors settled everything down, Giselle asked one where they took Winter, Being a couple years older than Winter she had no problem sneaking away from the Children's Home to go be with her friend. With everything going on they didn't even notice her leaving the premises.

Giselle hitched a ride to The Greater Baltimore Medical Center with an old man riding down the street. She sat in his rusty old truck holding her breath the whole ride. The smell was overbearing and she gagged continuously. When he let her out down the street from the hospital, the fresh air was inviting to her lungs. But that wasn't stopping her from running to the entrance quickly to get to Winter's side. She went to the security desk, got the information she needed, rushed to the elevators, and proceeded to Winter's room.

As the elevator made its way to the third floor, she exited and went towards where the guard directed her. As soon as she got there, she saw nurse after nurse leave out of

# The Secrets He Kept

Winter's room. She just knew it was serious what she had to go through and she got mad all over again.

"Is this Winter's room?" Giselle asked a nurse that just rushed out holding a bloody towel.

"Yes it is hunny, but you can't go in there right now, the doctor is still in there with the patient," the nurse said while she went right past her moving fast.

Giselle grabbed a chair and sat outside the room until she got word that she could go in. With all her thoughts running throughout her head, it took her back to that place she tried over and over to forget; the reason why she was living in the Children's Home and not with her parents.

*"Giselle, bring yo' ass here now little girl." Giselle thought to herself what the hell did I do now.*

*She tried her best to stay out her father's way while he was in one of his drunken rants.*

*"Here I come poppa."*

*"Where is your whore ass mother?" he yelled spilling some of his Jack Daniels on Giselle.*

*"I don't know poppa, she hasn't been here all day."*

*It wasn't a time when her mother was around. Heroin was becoming her only family and she left Giselle there to put up with her father's rage.*

*"I hate you and that whore. I don't even know why you were even born," her poppa roared at her, spittle flying everywhere.*

*Giselle just stepped back and let him get out everything he needed to say before he passed out from drinking.*

*"Where you going slut? Step back here!" He grabbed Giselle by her tiny wrist and twisted it hard before he sent her a backhand slap that made her fly into the wall.*

# The Secrets He Kept

"Please stop poppa," Giselle said before she tried to get up and run into her room.

Even with the half of gallon of whiskey he had in his system, he was still faster than her. He threw the thick glass that was still filled to the rim with the strong liquor, and it landed straight in the back of her head, which made her black out. He didn't stop there. He took off his belt and beat her without mercy. When that didn't satisfy his thirst of getting back at her mother for being who she was, he raped and beat her some more, pissed all over her, and tried to hang her in her room to end her life.

The liquor had taken a toll on him so his efforts were tripled the effect every time he looked at Giselle. He finally let Giselle's weak and bruised body fall to the floor and his body soon fell right on top of her. When she awoke and saw how battered her body was, she went to the bathroom, showered, and packed her bags. This was the last time she would ever step foot in the door of the only house she ever knew. While living on the streets for years, a 14 year old Giselle finally came to the Children's Home and has been there ever since.

Giselle snapped out her thoughts when she seen a doctor leave the room, she got out her chair to make sure it was ok to go in now.

"Hello sir, I'm Giselle and I'm Winter's friend from the home. Is it possible for me to go in and check on her now?" Giselle asked.

"Hi Giselle, my name is Doctor Cole, and yes you can see her, she has been asking about you and Abe since she got her," Doctor Cole smiled.

"Who is Abe, I don't know an Abe." Giselle was a bit confused as to who that was.

Since knowing Winter she never mentioned him.

"Maybe she can tell you that when you go in. I'll give you an hour but then she needs her rest," Doctor Cole told her.

"Thank you sir, I appreciate it." With that being said, she walked inside Winter's room and watched her fidget in her bed. She couldn't explain why she felt so close to her but she knew their friendship would last a long time.

# Chapter 18

Winter's wounds healed after being in the hospital for two weeks. Giselle and Doctor Cole never left her side once. He wanted to take her home with him then but was still in the process of getting the paperwork done with social services. After what happened at the Children's Home, he felt enough was enough. The child had been through too much and he only wanted to protect her from the world.

Winter sat at the room in her dorm room watching Giselle prance around in the mirror. Her hair was no longer fiery red, now it was some burnt orange color that had hints of yellow in it that made it look a little bit like the sun when it's about to set. She laughed at her friend while she danced to some house music she had never heard before. Giselle popped, locked, and broke it down. She was happy that Krystal was in Juvenile for what she had done to Winter. When Giselle finally got tired of dancing, she jumped on the bed to hug her friend.

"Get off me," Winter pushed Giselle in a playful manner.

"Girl, I can hug you, don't get all brand new on me." Giselle pushed Winter back and they both fell out laughing.

The door to their room opened and the girls got quiet at the director standing there slightly tapping her feet.

"You two are nerve wrecking," she said to Giselle and Winter both.

"Hi director Tims," spoke Winter.

"Yeah, how are you?" Giselle added.

"Well I am fine Miss Lady, but I need you to come with me because you have a visitor."

"Who?" the girls said in union.

# The Secrets He Kept

They looked at each other and laughed again. For some reason they were in a goofy mood. Giselle caught the strange look Ms. Tims was giving them and she abruptly stopped laughing.

"I mean which one of us have a visit?" Giselle asked.

"Winter." With that she turned on her heels.

Winter secretly wanted it to be Abe but she hasn't heard from him in God knows when, and even thought she was mad at him for not coming to see her or even trying to find out if she was alive, a girl can only hope. However, she knew all too well who was there; the only person in the world that knew she was there. Someone she had grown to love as a father and that was Doctor Cole.

"Can you tell Doctor Cole I will be down in a minute please?"

"Make it quick Winter, he is a busy man." The director left the two girls giggling on the bed.

"I wonder what he wants," Giselle said.

"Probably to see if I'm ok. He is a really good man, I want you to get to know him more," Winter admitted.

"I'll try Winter, but I can say one thing good about him is he is fine. I mean real fine too," Giselle cooed.

The girls laughed some more then Winter got up from her bed, checked herself out in the mirror, and left Giselle to go see what Doctor Cole wanted.

Winter walked into the family room and Doctor Cole was seated on a couch at the very back of the room. He kept crossing and un-crossing his legs. He looked dapper in a crisp white shirt with a tan and beige sweater on top of it, with a pair of jeans that fit him perfectly. When he noticed that Winter had come into the room, he stood and motioned for her to come over to join him. Winter's smile spread across

# The Secrets He Kept

her face as wide as it would go. When she got close to him, she gave him the biggest hug; his heart fluttered when she hugged him. This girl had changed something in him. Dealing with his career, he didn't have time for a family, but she had changed that in the little time that he has known her. She made him love again and now since things with social services were looking up, he was able to take her home with him next week.

"Hi Winter," he said while he pulled her out of his embrace.

"Hi Doctor Cole, how are you today?" Winter uttered.

"I am fine and you?" Doctor Cole stated.

"I'm good, so what brings you here?" Winter said while she sat down.

Doctor Cole sat across from her and straightened his collar on his shirt. He was so nervous and didn't know how she was going to take the news he was about to deliver.

"Well I came to ask you, Winter, some important questions. I know you have been through a lot these past few months and we had no luck at finding you a better home or even any family that could come get you. Now the time I have been your physician I have grown to love you as my own. I don't have any kids or a wife and I would like to change that. So what I am saying to you Winter is, I was wondering would you like to come live with me from now on and we could be a family... only if you want to there, is no pressure," Doctor Cole blurted out.

Winter stared at the doc and tears rolled down her face profusely. All she heard was be a family and everything else went in one ear and out the other. She jumped in the doc's arms and wrapped her arms around his neck way to tightly.

PLATINUM AND SAKEENA

117

# The Secrets He Kept

"I would love to be your daughter, when do I leave? Can Giselle come to?" She rumbled on with question after question not skipping a beat.

"You can leave next week. We will have to see what the state says about Giselle. She is a pretty awesome friend to you, but can you release my neck before you strangle me?" Doctor Cole laughed from the look on Winter's face when she realized what she was doing.

"I have to go tell Giselle the good news," Winter screamed ready to spread the news.

"I don't think you have to, turn around," Doctor Cole nodded.

When Winter turned around, she saw Giselle standing there with a slight grin on her face. She ran to her new best friend and hugged her tightly too.

"Oh Giselle, he wants me to be his daughter," Winter said with so much joy in her heart.

"I heard you kiddo, I am so happy for you," Giselle mumbled.

She was truly happy for her friend but also sad at the same time.

"He said you can come if the state let you, do you want to come? I don't want to lose you when I just found you." Winter held her breath waiting on an answer.

Giselle looked into Winter's eyes, placed her forehead on top of hers and let out a deep breath.

"Where you go I go Winter." Giselle let her tears fall.

She had never experienced this kind of love. She was grateful to have met Winter when she did.

Doctor Cole watched as the girls discussed how pretty their rooms were going to be. He silently laughed to himself and thought *what I'ma do with a teenage girl and one becoming one soon?*

He walked over to them and gave them both hugs.

"Well I have to go to work you two. Giselle, first thing in the morning I will put the paperwork in for you and hopefully they will let you leave with us next week. Now you both stay out of trouble, I'll see you soon," Doctor Cole announced sounding like a true father.

Doctor Cole gave them both kisses on the cheeks and exited. The girls watched from the window as he pulled off in his silver Benz. When the smoked cleared, they hopped up and down excitedly.

# Chapter 19

Abe couldn't live with his self for going along with Tristin's plan. He should have never allowed that to happen. He should have fought for her or died trying. But he couldn't think like that anymore. Now that she is safe and now that the doctor knows what's going on, he doesn't have to look over her anymore. Getting Doctor Cole on his side was a fight in itself. He only implicated his brother and his gang in the shooting. He couldn't tell him he had a hand in it too. Once he gave him the run down on how important the situation was,  and him and the doc devised a plan for the doc to take custody of her so she could live out the rest of her life without a care in the world.

Abe was heartbroken. The only friend he had in this world, he would never get to see again; the only girl he ever loved in this world, he would never get to let her know how he truly felt. From the day of his last visit with Winter, days had turned into months. He just couldn't face her and decided to stay away from her. He would never forgive his self if he led Tristin to her, so he just stayed away.

Doc kept him in the loop of how Winter was doing. He just hoped his life would turn out to be as half as good as hers will. Sleeping from one abandon building to the other, his hopes wasn't that high about his life. Once he tried to find his mother by searching every crack house Baltimore had to offer, but she was nowhere to be found. Luckily for him, she was probably already dead somewhere with a needle hanging in her arm. Life was getting too hard to bear. He was running out of clean clothes and word on the streets is his brother and his gang was out looking for him. That was something he didn't want to run across.

# The Secrets He Kept

Tristin could be un-predictable. One minute he was a big brother, the other a stone-cold killer. A few days back, he almost ran into Greg at the hospital. He was glad that he didn't catch him. Now here he is laying on top of a dirty cardboard box hiding out from a gang. He was smelling like he hadn't washed his ass in years. He laid there with his arms folded under his head to support his neck, thinking of the one person he could talk to but dared not.

*"Why you always want to play checkers knowing I'm going to beat you?"* he asked Winter while he gave her a double jump to end the game.

*"Seriously Abraham, I let you beat me. I like the way your eyes sparkle when you think you're beating me,"* Winter responded.

*"Come on now Winter, I can beat you with my eyes closed."*

*Winter just shook her head and reset the board so they could play another game.*

*"Are you ready to play again?"* she asked.

*"No I'm tired of checkers, let's just do some homework."*

Abe was taken out of his thoughts by a loud bang coming from the basement of the building he was sleeping in. He sat up from his spot and just listened for a sound. *Bam!* There it was again. This time Abe got up to his feet grabbing his little .22. His mind was telling him to run the other way but his body led him in the direction towards the noise.

As he walked closer to the commotion, he started to hear voices. It was a man and a woman's voice, but Abe froze when hear heard the man scream.

"Bitch I told you I was going to find you. Why you took my shit? I know it was you," the man yelled.

# The Secrets He Kept

"I'm so sorry Tristin. I'ma pay you back," Tracie screamed.

Abe couldn't believe his luck. All the while he was trying to hide from his big brother, what were the chances he would show up in the same part of town Abe was in? He watched quietly in hopes that Tristin and his mother would just leave.

"Bitch I'm not trying to hear that. You made me lose a lot of money behind your unfit ass." Tristin snapped landing a couple more blows to the stomach of Tracie.

It hurt Abe to his heart to watch his brother beating on his mother like she was a rag doll. He gripped his hand around his gun. The more his mother cried out the madder he got.

"Tristin please stop. I'm sorry. I got a job now. I can pay you back next week when I get my check," Tracie cried.

"You think I'm supposed to believe that?" Tristin huffed. "Run me my motherfucking money. I'm not playing with you."

"I don't have it. All I have is my money to eat with," Tracie lied.

Hell, she only had money from her last trick to get her next high.

Tristin took a step back and just shook his head. Having a mother like Tracie taught him how not to love a person. She was never there for him or his brother. He raised his gun, aiming at Tracie's head. Killing her would rid the world of an unfit mother. He pulled the hammer back placing his finger on the trigger.

"Wait no. Please son don't do this. What will happen to your brother if you kill me? I promise to pay you back every penny of your money." Tracie was now in tears.

She had never seen this look in her son's eyes. She knew she was about to die.

"Bitch, he will be better off without you. You keep that money and I hope you enjoyed the dope. See you on the other side," Tristin hissed.

He closed his eyes. Even though he was about to kill his mother, he didn't want to see the sad look in her eyes.

POW! POW! POW! Three shots was fired hitting its intended target.

"Ugh!" Tristin screamed out in pain. He quickly opened his eyes and fired back at the dark figure shooting at him. He ducked for cover trying not to get hit again. His right arm was killing him.

Abe was glad his aim was accurate. After shooting his brother, he took off running. He wasn't sure if Tristin knew who he was and wasn't about to stick around to see. He ran for dear life. Although his mother wasn't there for him much, he still loved her and didn't want any harm to come to her. He could hear Tristin yelling from behind him but he never looked back.

Abe finally realized what a true monster his brother was. He hated him for what he had made him do to Winter and he hated him for all the hell he put him through. He didn't know how but he had to get out of town. He ran full speed through somebody's yard and hopped the fence. He continued his run until he was out of breath.

# Chapter 20

It was time for both Winter and Giselle to leave the Children's Home and start their new lives with Doctor Cole. When he pulled up with the social worker, the girls were already packed and ready to go. He walked in with a grin from ear to ear, greeted the girls, gave them a hug, and took their luggage from them. Since Winter didn't have much, she only handed him a duffle bag. The social worker gave the girls a once over and let them leave with the doc to their new place of residence.

The car ride was smooth and long. Doctor Cole lived an hour away in an upscale neighborhood. When the girls saw the big beautiful houses pass by, their mouths dropped open. All their lives they had to struggle and for once it were starting to feel like their gloomy lives would be filled with promise. Finally he stopped at a two-car garage, and next to it was a big, stone house with large bay windows, from the first floor to the roof. He pulled in the garage and let the girls out.

"Welcome to your new home ladies."

Nothing they ever did in their tiny lives compared to this journey they were headed on now.

"Thanks Dr. C," Winter and Giselle said together.

"Well if you girls walk to that door to your left, you can enter the house. From there you can either share a room or find one to fit you."

The girls looked at each other and ran to find the prettiest room they could find. They planned on sharing a room until they were tired of looking at each other.

Doctor Cole grabbed their luggage and followed the girls into the house, where he saw them racing all around their new surroundings. They looked happy and he was glad he was the one to put that smile upon their faces. He dropped the bags in the living room and fell down in his recliner. Today he was going to do nothing but rest and let the girls get acquainted with their house.

Later that night after the commotion died down, he ordered pizza for the three of them; it was going on ten that night. He had to get them re-registered in a different school and go to a shift at the hospital. Parenthood was new to him but he was determined to pull it off.

"After you both finish your food, we need to get you both in the bed. We have a busy day ahead of us."

"OK Dr. C" Giselle said. She picked up her plate and headed to the kitchen.

"I want to thank you for helping us both. I know you didn't have to do it," Winter exclaimed.

"It was my pleasure Winter, you don't have to thank me at all. You girls will bring more meaning into my life and I'm hoping we all can be a family starting now. You guys don't have to call me Doctor Cole, you can call Bret," Doctor Cole smiled.

"I hope the same thing too," Winter said.

Winter picked up her plate walked to Doctor Cole gave him a tight hug and headed towards the kitchen.

She walked past Giselle and sat her plate in the sink.

"Are you ok Winter?" Giselle asked.

"Yeah I'm ok, I just hope we don't disappoint him. He didn't have to take us in and give us this lifestyle we will be living. Sometimes I think it's too good to be true," Winter admitted.

"Never look a gift horse in the mouth Winter. You're right, he didn't have to do this for us but he did, so let's enjoy it while it lasts."

"You're right, are you ready to head to bed?" Giselle questioned.

"Bed? Don't that sound strange? Not cot, not concrete or dorm with six girls but bed... yes, I am ready to go lay in my bed," Giselle laughed.

The girls passed out as soon as their heads touched the pillow. He watched by their door at the slight snoring they both did, they were alike in some ways but different in others. To him Winter was sensitive and smart. Giselle was headstrong and determined, but together they were going to give the world something to reckon with and with his guidance, both these girls were going to become great. He walked towards their beds, pulled their covers up, turned off the light, and went back down stairs into his office.

Doctor Cole walked to his bar and poured him a glass of twenty-year-old scotch, sat on his couch and opened a medical journal. Moments later, his phone rang. After he looked at the unknown number on the caller ID, he finally answered on the third ring.

Caller: Is she safe?

Doctor Cole: Yes she is safe. Are you sure you don't want to come see her? She has been asking about you.

Caller: No, I can't let anyone know she is still alive. Her life is in danger; just take care of her for me.

Doctor Cole: But I can help you both, just let me help you.

Caller: You already did by giving her the best life possible. You can do something for me though.

Doctor Cole: Name it.

Caller: I need some money to get out of town. Things here are getting bad for me.

Doctor Cole: Sure. Where are you? I can bring it to you.

Caller: No, no, just pay for me a bus ticket. I'm using a pay phone. I will call you back in an hour for the conformation number.

Doctor Cole: If that's what you want. Just make sure you take care of yourself and if you ever need anything you have the number.

Caller: Will do. After this I won't be contacting you anymore.

Doctor Cole looked at the phone again as the dial tone buzzed loudly out of the receiver. He wondered what and why was someone was hunting this girl. What could she have possibly done for someone to want to kill her? He vowed to his new friend he would keep her safe and he intended to do just that. After the things he saw that she had been through, nothing in this world was going to take his daughter away from him, or nobody. He thought about asking Detective Gonzales did he have any new leads but his friend advised him not to do it.

So much secrecy. One day he was going to get to the bottom of this, until that time came, he had two girls soundly asleep in his spare bedroom waiting for someone to give them the life they deserved. Tomorrow is a new day, a fresh start for the both of them. He wondered how their lives were going to affect his but put it right back out his head as it came in. It really didn't matter; he needed them and they needed him.

Doctor Cole pressed a couple buttons on his computer and then shut it down. He walked back to the bar and poured himself another drink, turned off his office lights and headed to his bedroom. He went to his dresser, pulled out a pair of cotton pajamas, set them on the bed and walked into his full bathroom with a shower and separate Jacuzzi tub. He wanted to relax but opted out on using the tub, and headed to his huge marble walk-in shower, turned the shower on to a nice temperature, stripped naked and stepped in.

He was in deep thought when the arm wrapped around him; the waterfall that came out his showerhead had him in a daze. Without looking he spoke to the intruder.

"I told you don't come here today Madison," Doctor Cole sighed.

"But baby, I needed to see you. I thought I meant something to you," Madison cooed.

"You have to go, and leave my key on my nightstand," Doctor Cole whispered.

Doctor Cole turned around and looked at the black beauty with the perky breasts standing before him. Even though he wanted to taste one, he knew she had to leave.

"Come on Cole, let me stay," Madison pouted.

"Didn't I tell you I have two daughters that I have to worry about? They are my world now and you just don't fit in."

He walked towards her, wrapped his hand around her throat and pushed his penis right between her wet thighs.

"You want this don't you?" he said still choking her and grinding his long shaft on her. "But you can't get it anymore, now get the fuck out my house before I throw you out!"

He turned off the shower, grabbed a towel to wrap around his body, and stepped out and dragged her out with him.

"I can't understand after six months you can do me like this."

"Well understand this." He walked her into his bedroom, made her get dressed and snatched his keys way from her.

"Don't call me, don't come around me, we are through since you don't know your fucking place."

"Fuck you Cole!" Madison screamed and stormed out his bedroom just to run into Winter.

"Oh, so you the little bitch who took my place? Fuck you and your new daddy," Madison seethed.

Winter stood in shock as the woman stood there fuming at her for no reason.

"Madison, if you ever in your life talk to my daughter like that again, I will fucking kill you. Now get the fuck out my life," Cole screamed as he watched in horror at how she spoke to Winter.

Madison knew he wasn't playing. She rushed down the stairs as fast as she could and got the fuck out of dodge.

"Are you ok Winter?"

"Yeah Dr. C, I've been through worst," Winter admitted.

"Do you need for me to get you anything?"

"No I'm cool, I'm just gone head back to bed. We do have a busy day ahead of us and I can't wait to start it."

"I agree, we both have busy days. Goodnight Winter and I am sorry you had to witness that."

"That's alright pops, goodnight."

Winter went into her bedroom and lay back down. Doctor Cole stood in the middle of the hallway stuck on what he had just heard.

*She called me pops; damn I could get use to that.*

He exited back into his room and lay down. Tomorrow was the day his life really started. The day he becomes a parent to two beautiful young girls. This was the best thing he ever did besides go to medical school. Leaving Madison to fend for herself had him thinking he shouldn't just leave it like that. He grabbed his robe and hurriedly walked to his door to catch up with her. When he arrived at the door, he swung it open only to catch her speeding off out of his doorway. Being the gentleman that he is, he decided to give her a call in the morning.

Charles knew following Madison was going to lead him to her son, but to see her leave out of her boyfriend house pissed him off even more. He waited until she got down the road some before he made his move. Either she gives up her son's location or she finds her a new place to call home; and he didn't care that, that home was a shallow grave.

Madison pissed at how Bret just treated her, searched her purse for her cell to call her son. But some jackass behind her had his high beams on blast and it blinded her. Charles blew his horn and rammed the back of Madison car, sending her spinning off the road into a ditch. He hopped out the car and rushed to the driver's side. With his pistol close to his side, he banged on Madison's window until she raised it down. He raised the pistol to her head.

"Now since you find yourself in this jam there is only one way out... show me where your son is," Charles hissed.

**To Be Continued...**

**Also coming soon by Author Sakeena Raheem...**

# Chapter 1

When I opened my door the sun was shining bright as hell in my face. I took my right hand and used it as a shield to block the light out so I could check the mailbox. When I stuck my hand in, I pulled out several envelopes containing junk mail and bills. It was a beautiful day for it to be the beginning of May; Chicago's weather really didn't break until the middle of June. I made my way down the rest of the porch and took a seat on the very last step, opened my mail and discarded what I didn't need. Since all my bills were paid up anyway, the notices that they sent weren't important to me. My head tilted back to catch a much needed tan. Even though my brown skin didn't need one, the warmth was welcoming nonetheless. A slight breeze slid through and lifted up the bottom of the long, flowing summer dress I was wearing. I laughed when the thought of it blowing all the way up and the people that was walking up and down the street noticed that I wasn't wearing any panties, but I quickly held it down with my hand. I never wear under garments in the summer time. I felt like that was the time to let everything breathe. Only thing that I was upset about was I didn't have a man to share my nudeness with. I really wasn't upset. I had friends I will occasionally go see but never one to really call my own. At first I thought it was me, but it couldn't have been. I was too cool of a female to still be single. I had a nice shaped body, a slight pudge in the belly department, but not too much, a big ass and pretty face. Now I wasn't and will never be a Victoria's Secret model, but I wasn't ugly.

I wasn't going to dwell on that right now though. My next door neighbor waved me to come over while he watered his grass, as he called out my name. I just shook my head because I knew this old man wanted to be more than just neighbors with me.

"Carmen check it out, I got something to tell you," Bruce yelled me over. I stood up, straightened out my long, black dress and walked over to him.

"Hey Bruce, what it do old man?" I answered back.

"Nothing much just trying to get some of this good weather we are receiving. You know how the city's weather acts; today it's warm and the next we gone have a blizzard." I laughed at his statement because he was right. Chicago had the most bizarre weather patterns.

"So what's on your agenda for the weekend, it's Friday and I know you are not sitting in the house?" He kept asking me questions and Lord knows I hate being asked questions, but I amused him anyway.

"Well first I'm going to buy me a bottle and then I'm going to sit on this porch and see what these fools who stay on this block do to entertain me," I answered back.

"Ok Carmen let me get back to this poor excuse of a lawn."

"Alright," I said before I walked back and sat on the last step of my porch again.

I sat there and watched everybody's actions. People were moving so fast. Some guys were standing on the corner just talking, about three girls stood at the bus stop waiting on the bus, kids played tag and others played football in the field. This was a beautiful day outside. I didn't blame no one for taking advantage of it. I turned my head to the right and that's when I saw him. It was like he was designed just for me. I just knew he wasn't from around here because I have never seen him before. He was at least six feet tall, light skinned but not high yellow. He walked like he had a bounce in his step, but not really a bounce. His left foot pushed up off the ground while his right stayed flat on the ground. His light brown eyes were sparkling, and his smile was breathtaking. He wore an all-white t-shirt, backpack and black pants. I could see him nodding his head up and down to the music coming from his headphones. When he finally passed me, he gave me a head nod and kept walking. My heart skipped several fucking beats when he did that. I wanted to say hi back but for the first time the cat had my damn tongue. Abruptly I stood up. I thought for a second to go talk to him before he gets in one of these cars and you never see him again, but he walked past every car and never tried to open one. If he lived on this block or any block around here, why have I never seen him? This was very intriguing. I definitely was going to get to the bottom of this; I was determined to have him.

I rushed up to my mystery man and played off an accidently stumble so my body could brush up against his. He caught me at the right angle; his long hands gripped my body close to his. I gave him the best smile I could muster.

"Are you alright shorty?" He asked me.

"Yeah I'm good, my bad. I wasn't watching where I was going and lost my footing," I replied back to him, which was one of my best lies I ever came up with. I stood up straight and straightened out my dress before I got lost in those beautiful brown eyes again.

"No problem sweetie, my name's Thomas, what's yours?" His deep voice had my juices sliding down my leg every time he spoke.

"My name is Carmen," I retorted back and gave him my hand so I could give him a handshake.

# The Secrets He Kept

We shook hands and our eyes never left each other. For a moment there I thought he would never give me my hand back and I could feel it start to sweat. I eased it away slowly, wiped my sweaty palms on my dress and walked away.

He gave me one last smile and continued on his way. I could feel the need for him run through me and was mad I let this once in a lifetime chance just walk away from me. I wanted to turn around so badly wrap my arms around his waist and kiss him like I have never kissed before. I sat on my porch and closed my eyes leaned my head back and sulked at the way I just acted. How could I just let someone as fine as him get away so quickly, but pushed the thought out my mind because he was too damn sexy not to have a girlfriend. The sun was getting to hot to bare so I opted out of sitting on my porch to go back inside my house to get rid of this feeling I was having deep in my love nest the only thing that was going to make me feel better was my best friend Michael the vibrator.

When I opened my eyes Thomas was standing in front of me smiling hard as if he had just read my thoughts and I blushed. My face turned beet red and couldn't hide just how embarrassed I really was.

"I forgot to tell you Carmen you have a beautiful smile so I came back, I'm sorry if I interrupted you".

A laughed escaped my lips.

"Thank you Thomas, but you didn't interrupt me I was just going back inside to get out of this heat".

"I am in a rush today but I would love to see you again Carmen if you would let me, here is my number call me sometimes". Thomas said while he wrote his number on my arm.

"I could have gotten you some paper".

"I didn't need any; maybe I just wanted to touch your soft skin again?"

Now why would he say that the man hasn't even entered me and I came just off his words and touch. If he could do that with no problem I would hate to see how he would have my body react when I let him inside me.

"Ok Thomas I'm going to let you go I know you have some work to do and me as well I'll give you a call one day this week.

"Ok Carmen don't forget". He said before he walked off.

I raced up my stairs ran through my empty house to my room grabbed Michael out my toy box and went to work on my pussy. I was so wet my bed felt like I wasted a gallon of water on me. This man was going to be the death of me.

# CHAPTER 2

Weeks had passed and I still couldn't muster up the nerves to call Thomas, I didn't know why, he had everything I looked for in a man he was tall, handsome had a job and went to school studying to become a chef. I know you wondering how I knew that and I have only talked to him once. But after that day we talked on my porch it became my routine to accidently be outside when he was leaving school dressed in his chef uniform coming home and when he left to go to work in the afternoon. He was always nice when he walked past always speaking and me acting as goofy as I can. Sometimes I wondered why I didn't just call him and get it out the way but deep down I knew why. I had just gotten out a five year relationship with a friend who turned into my lover. Anthony was a little shorter than me dark skinned and a complete Jock he was a running back in college and a personal trainer at a gym downtown. Our relationship was a good one more ups then downs but then he moved back home to St. Louis out of nowhere and broke my heart. We kept in touched and had a long distance relationship for a while but then he did the unthinkable and had a baby on me. He did what every other weak nigga did try to talk his way out of it. "Carmen I don't love her I love you, I told her to get rid of it but she won't". How could you love me and knowingly get another woman pregnant. We still cool though and we are still good friends. But let me get back to Thomas I learned he lived down the street a few blocks from my house as I was taking one of my daily walks through my hood he was in his yard showing his chiseled slightly hairy chest pushing his lawn mower up and down his lawn. As I walked past he gave me that sexy ass smile that made butterflies flutter in my stomach. I quickly gave him a head nod and kept on my journey trying not to pay him that much attention knowing damn well I wanted to be that rag he wiped his sweat off with just to be close to his body. Now I'm just here holding my cell in my hand debating if I would call him or Anthony, I wanted to speak to my friend but I also wanted to hear how Thomas voice sounded on the phone. This bullshit ass game I was playing was getting old my mother always said either you piss or get off the pot. But I didn't want to rush this maybe I was more scared than I thought but I know I didn't call either one. I sat on my bed and opened up my book Dirty Red by Vickie Stringer I've been reading. I lay back on my bed propped my back up against my wall and settled myself in. Once I opened up to the page I left off on my fingers found its way right back between my legs dammit my mind was drifting off back to Thomas. I needed him in the worst way but right now my fingers should suffice, my book dropped to my side and I let my fingers explore the inside of my pussy I envisioned Thomas was there fondling my breasts taking each one in his mouth like a ripe peach he just picked from a tree and sucked on letting the juices flow freely from his mouth. Damn why did this man have such a hold over me and I only really spoke to him once. When my fingers found their destination to my g spot I wasted no time cumming all over them I tasted my own nectar if I wasn't comfortable tasting myself how could I ask a man do it. With my clothes soaked with my pussy juices I walked to my closet and grabbed my short midnight silky blue robe my Aunt got me as a birthday gift. Threw it over my shoulder and went into my bathroom to clean myself up. The hot water was refreshing as I let my shower take me into another world. A world where there was only Thomas and I making love on everything we could.

# The Secrets He Kept

Tonight was the night I was going to get my man no more games, no more hi and bye just him and me face to face. I hopped out the shower after I scrubbed my body with my bath and body works shower gel wrapped a towel around my body ran to my room and grabbed my phone.

"Yo Adrian meet me at my house at nine I need to have a damn drink and a big one". I said into the phone to my best friend when she picked up

"I'll be there at 8:30 so be ready I need one myself and I have some gossip I got to tell you" Adrian boasted.

"Aight bitch hurry up and get ready cause we bout to turn the city up tonight" I hurriedly ended the call before she went into one of her gossip rants I loved Adrian but that girl was destined to be a news anchor cause she told people business better than the news. Adrian has been my girl since grammar school that was thirty years ago and we still rocking till this day. Adrian was shorty, dark skinned with a Brazilian weave that flowed past her small waist and medium ass. She was out spoken and ready to pop a bitch in the mouth without any hesitation.

I grabbed my Johnson and Johnson baby oil off my dresser and positioned myself in front of my full length mirror and rubbed myself down with the oily liquid. I oiled every part of my body and when My fingers found their way back between my thighs I laughed to myself knowing if I kept feeling how warm it felt down there I would end up playing with Michael and I had other plans, I shook off the feeling I had stirring and returned to the task at hand. I walked into my closet which was crammed with clothes some new with tags still on them and some old I just didn't have the heart to throw away. I was a clothes hoarder and loved every piece of fabric I had in there. Since it was unusually warm for May I picked up a black bandage dress I got from forever 21 and a pair of closed toe black wedges. I took off my head scarf and let my short bob fall into place. I sprayed my favorite perfume Wild honeysuckle over me and sat on my bed and read my book until it was time for Adrian to come pick me up.

Adrian pulled up just in time she sat in front of my house and blew her horn like I was deaf and couldn't hear it.

I hated when she acted ratchet but she was my best friend and I loved her.

"Hurry up and bring yo ass Carmen" Adrian yelled at me while I locked my door.

"Bitch here I come with yo simple as. I yelled back at her.

As soon as I made my way to her car and hopped in all you could smell was the finest loud Chicago had to offer.

"Damn bitch you need to clean yo damn car got lil bugs crawling around my new shoes" I screamed over the music she had blasting thru her speakers.

"Girl boo, I practically live out this muthafucka and Josh bitch ass won't go get it detailed for me" Adrian screamed turning her system all the way up.

"Whatever bitch let's go to the liquor store I need me some 1800 and a bottle of wine". We pulled off from in front of my house and headed straight towards the neighborhood liquor store. I really wish she would clean her car and depending on her bitch ass nigga to do anything to go out his way to help her would be like waiting for Jesus to come back. Josh was a light skinned nigga that had good hair and pretty eyes and thought the world revolved around him. Adrian could do so much better but she loved his funky drawls But Josh and I was like oil and water we just didn't mix and every chance I got to let him know that I did.

# The Secrets He Kept

We got to 200 liquors located about a half mile away from my house, parked and hopped out looking like the sexy vixens we were. Adrian had on a pair of black jean dukes that made her ass look gorgeous a white see thru shirt and a leather black bra and a pair of blinged out wedges to complete her outfit. Adrian switched her way into the store bumping into some hood rat that had way too much glue on her lashes.

"Damn my bad shorty" Adrian said while she smirked and I laughed as the hood rat looked like she wanted to get out her body with my friend so I interjected.

"Look excuse my friend she needs a little more fiber in her diet she is harmless though". I told her to calm her down before Adrian did a 180 and knocked her out.

The young girl just looked at me and smacked her lips and stormed out the door. Adrian busted out laughing getting the attention of the other customers in the store. I grabbed her arm and led her to the fridge where they stored the wine.

"Why every time we go out you got to start some shit" I scolded her.

"Carmen that bitch wasn't hitting on shit I got this, but why yo ass always want to be captain save a hoe. Tell me that hell". Adrian said with way too much sarcasm.

"You know what, we ain't even finna start this mess I'm ready to get drunk have some cutie feel on this ass and party. I opened the fridge grabbed me a big bottle of Livingston sangria and walked towards the register, gently sat the bottle on the counter and asked the clerk to give me a half gallon of 1800 tequila. Tonight was gone be a turn up night and Adrian was not gone be the reason why my temper flared, only thing that was gone make me mad was if

# The Secrets He Kept

I couldn't bring home a sexy muthafucka ready to take this pussy down.

# CHAPTER 3

We opted out of going inside a hot ass club, we both decided to just park down the street from my house and see what the hood had to offer since they was all outside littering the streets anyway.

We sat on 49th Princeton and the block was jumping they had everyone out enjoying the little heat wave we had. Bitches had on the littlest shit they could find from their last year wardrobe some looked decent while others didn't even notice they were downright tacky. A couple of the young ladies I did sometimes hang with came over and joined Adrian and I in our festivities. I cracked open both bottles and poured me up a double shot and a tall cup of wine. While I watched all the guys shoot their best game to some of the females I couldn't lie I was having way more fun here than sitting in a boring club and since the violence in Chicago has consumed my city I felt safer that I was sitting a few blocks down from my house hell and since I could remember Adrian kept a pistol under her driver seat. She wasn't scared to blow back at no one I guess growing up in the heart of Englewood would do that to you.

My favorite song When I walk thru by Rich Homie Quan came blasting out Adrian's radio system I stood half way in the street and started to two step to it I let his lyrics take me away.

Yeah, hey man where my real niggas at in this muh' fucker man?

You feel me? Do the real nigga walk through for me hey

[Hook]

# The Secrets He Kept

I be feeling like the man when I walk through
Ain't stunting what you saying when I walk through
I got all these hoes staring when I walk through
I done made a few bands when I walk through
Watch me, watch me, hey, watch me walk through
Watch me, watch me, hey, watch me walk through
Watch me, watch me, hey, watch me walk through
I done made a few bands when I walk through

I done made a few bands when I walk through
People I don't know naw I don't talk to
Me and Problem in this bitch, he a boss too
Sitting at the round table making boss moves
I done walk thru with Gucci on my feet
Who got more money, you or me?
I'mma walk through usually with my nigga best
believe
That I got the tool on me I done snuck passed
security
What the fuck, do you need glasses just to see
Me when I'm coming full speed, got that V12 running
And I'mma jump the fence if I see 12 coming
Even if I were blind, I could still smell money
I can't trust no outside niggas, they could tell on me
I'm the alphabet boy 'cause I keep an L on me
I smoke good, throwing up my set in your hood,
nigga

Man I had the whole hood grooving to my antics it
was one big party until I finally let my head up and made eye
contact to no other than Thomas staring at me even at one
in the morning that man eyes sparkled. He gave me a wide
smile and I retreated back to Adrian car as fast as I could and
stood there like I didn't even know him. He wanted to walk

over and talk to me I could see it in his mannerisms as much as I wanted him to be next to me I never let my business hit the streets. That was something I learned at an early age, if they don't know always keep them guessing.

He stood by his iron gate with a plastic cup of white liquid in his hand talking to some of the guys that lived in his building, he smiled at me most times and the other times he pleaded with me to come talk to him without any words being spoken. And every time I looked at him out the corner of my eye and another girl walked passed him throwing pussy his way I got jealous and rage filled my heart so I took it out on the liquor and by three that night I was fucked up yelling at Adrian to take me home.

"Adrian, Adrian", I yelled at her slurring my words and almost tripping over my own two feet.

"Carmen, damn I hear you bitch, what? She reiterated with a snap of her neck.

"Man I need to go home I'm way too drunk to still be out here" Most people was still out enjoying themselves or I thought they was cause now I was seeing double. I laughed at my own self as I pointed and counted all 12 people I still saw outside.

"Come on Carmen let's go grab some gas and something to eat you will feel better than" Adrian came over to my side and ushered me into the backseat of her stinky ass car.

I scooted myself over as much as I could and held my breath until she hopped in and let down her window. Once she was in and started the car I was on her ass about Josh ole bitch ass.

"Bitch you need to tell that nigga either clean this muthafucka or buy you a new one" I yelled with her with Laughter in my voice.

# The Secrets He Kept

"Carmen shut the fuck up please, she begged me, I don't want to hear about his ass tonight, or how you dislike him, she put her seat belt on and put the car in drive checked her mirror and pulled off still trying to put me in my place. Now we finna go grab some gas and some food and I'm finna drop yo drunk ass off".

That bitch was the only person in the world that I let talk to me like that I took that shit in stride and passed out in her back seat that was the last thing I remembered that night.

**** 

I awoke undressed like usual I loved sleeping naked but the only thing that peaked my interests was that I was not alone. I couldn't believe I let this strange man in my house and not to mention my bed that shit was a no no. If I hooked up with any nigga and I rarely did he would be only allowed to take me to a hotel. I hit the snooze button on my TV and the news popped up with the time that read 5:45 am. Then I shook the nervousness out my body and lowered the covers that were over the mystery man head. To my surprise it was Thomas and he was naked as well. Several thoughts ran throughout my head, how in the world did he get here? Why does he smell so good? I hope he don't think I'm a hoe. Shit I silently screamed this man gone think I'm a hoe. As soon as I was about to remove myself from this predicament he woke up and grabbed my arm.

He looked at me first than the blinds.

"Good morning Carmen" he sang with that deep baritone voice

"Umm good morning Thomas" I stuttered

He stretched those long strong arms up over his head and let out a deep breath, he sat up and let his back rest against my wall, all while I sat there still in shock.

# The Secrets He Kept

"You don't have to look at me like that" He laughed at me

"I know I was drunk last night so can you please tell me what happened?

He laughed a hearty laugh this time, but what was strange was what he did next, he pulled me back towards him stared at me with those pretty light brown eyes, picked me up and sat me on his lap.

"What we did last night is what we are about to do again for the third time" was all he said before I felt his huge dick come to life. He placed his hard meaty shaft in my hands and my mouth began to salivate at the sight of it, it had the most intoxicating mushroom head the veins pulsated like a heartbeat every time he had me stroke it my pussy juices started to flow down his leg and he bit his lip making me even hungrier to have him inside me. I lifted up and placed his member where it needed to be at this moment, it glided in with ease I tightened my muscles around his shaft and he moaned like it was the best pussy he been in for a while. I rode him gently as he palmed my ass cheeks sending my body in convulsions. I don't know why but I came abruptly, he smiled at me and devoured my mouth with his sweet tasting tongue that sent my body to its next orgasm. We went toe for toe with each other for the next forty minutes I came at least seven times and still had more to give, my vibrator Michael never made me feel this good. When he finally busted he came inside me with full force digging his fingernails into my ass cheeks pushing his member as deep as my pussy would allow it to go we passed out in each other arms and fell fast asleep soon after.

# The Secrets He Kept

**Also coming soon by Platinum...**

"Jazmine! What is wrong with that damn baby?" Debbie yelled stumbling into the house.

She had had one drink to many and could barely walk. She wobbled over to her couch and flopped down. She kicked off her shoes and rested her head back on the couch. She still didn't get an answer from Jazz.

"Jazmine! I know you hear that damn baby crying." Debbie yelled.

She waited for another five minutes and baby Jaloni was still screaming his poor little lungs out. She got to her feet slowly. She took her time to stand straight up. She knew then she was drunk and needed to lay down. She walked down to her daughter's room. She pushed opened the door and could see baby Jaloni in his crib and Jazz was in her bed sound asleep.

Debbie lifted her right foot and kicked the bed with all her might. Jazz still didn't budge. Debbie reached over and slapped Jazz as hard as she could. Jazz shot up straight up in the bed.

"Get your ass up and get that damn baby." Debbie snapped.

"Ma he won't stop crying. I tried everything. I think something is wrong with him. Can you take me to the hospital?" Jazz sleepily asked.

She looked at the clock on her nightstand and it was passed four in the morning. She had only been to sleep for an hour. She caught a little break from Jaloni when he dozed off about two-forty five.

"Girl do you see what time it is? I'm not going anywhere. You betta shut him up so I can get some sleep." Debbie argued.

"But ma, I tried it all. I think he's running a fever or something. You don't have to stay up there with us. Can you just drop us off? Please." Jazz begged.

"My car ain't moving no more tonight. If you think he needs to be seen you need to call that sorry ass baby daddy of yours to come take you." Debbie uttered.

"I did but he still aint came over here yet." Jazz ranted.

"Welp I don't know what to tell you then. If he can't wait until I get up in the morning call 9-1-1. Your ass wasn't worried about that damn baby while you was out doing only God knows what with that sorry ass nigga." Debbie finalized before she walked away hitting the wall on her way out.

Jazz was out of options. She couldn't understand how her mother could treat her and her son the way she do. She felt like Debbie didn't care about them. In that moment she made up her mind that, that would be the last night staying under her mother roof. She couldn't take it anymore.

"Jazz I ain't going to tell you again. Shut the baby up or y'all got to go. I got a damn headache." Debbie hollered from her bedroom door.

Jazz hurried over to the crib. She yanked Jaloni up out of his crib and started rocking him harder and harder. She was so frustrated and didn't know what to do. She grabbed his bottle and shoved it into his mouth. Walking over to the dresser and turned on her radio. The tunes coming from the radio was soothing the baby. She turned on the night light and off the big light. She sat Indian style on the bed and rocked Jaloni until she watched him close his eyes.

Jazz reached for her cell phone. She pressed send and waited for Jarrett to answer. The phone rung five times before it went to his voicemail. She redialed his number over and over. The last time she left him a lengthy message, *Jarrett you are a piece of work. Our baby is sick and you out doing whatever you want to. I hate you. I know you seeing someone else but it's ok. I'm done with your bullshit and lies. Don't you ever call me again. As soon as I get enough money up I'm taking my baby and we are out of here. Don't look for us cause we won't be looking for you. I hope you meet somebody that will treat and misuse you like you did me. Bye creep!*

Jazz hit end on her cell and felt like a weight had been lifted off her shoulders. She didn't know she had the strength in her to break it off with him but she was tired of him dogging her. She kissed Jaloni on the forehead and promise him she wouldn't let anything happen to him.

Jazz hummed to the tune of the song. Before she knew it her and baby Jaloni was asleep.

****

Jazz was jolted out of her sleep yet again. This time by Debbie and a police Officer. She got up off the bed as slow as she could not to wake Jaloni. "Ma what's going on here?"

"This Officer needs to talk with you. I told him you was with that baby daddy of yours last night." Debbie said.

"Ma no I wasn't. I was with Kiyara for a lil bit and then I came back home." Jazz told her.

"You are such a big liar. You told me you was going to hang with them knuckle heads. Give me your damn phone." Debbie barked.

"Why? I didn't do nothing and I'm not lying. We was at Kiyara's house and then we walked over to Trizzey's house but they wasn't there so I walked home." Jazz repeated.

She didn't know what was going on but was scared.

"I said give me the God damn phone. Do it and do it now." Debbie yelled.

The Officer just stood back and watched the two interact. He was just there for a few questions. He wasn't there to tell the young black fine woman how to chastise her child. Watching her being so stern with her teenage daughter was turning him on in the worst way.

Jazz looked from the Officer and her mother, she could see she wasn't going to get any help so she passed over her cell phone and then crossed her arms across her chest. She watched as Debbie went through her cell phone.

"As I expected you talked to him last night twice." Debbie shook her head.

"Yes I talked to him last night but I didn't see him. Dang you act like it's a big deal. He's my baby daddy for God sakes." Jazz murmured.

"Om Officer what time did you say you found him?" Debbie asked not taking her eyes off her daughter.

"It was about five this morning." The Officer spoke up.

"Well would you look at this, she called him at four-thirty and talked to him for let see, three minutes and nine seconds." Debbie announced.

"And? What you don't want me talking to him now? What is going on here?" Jazz ranted.

"I'll take it from here Mrs...." The Officer stopped and waited for her name.

"That's Ms. Lang. I'm not married." Debbie smiled at him.

"Ok Ms. Lang do you mind if I speak to your daughter alone?" The Officer asked.

"Not at all Officer. Watch yourself with her as you can see she is a compulsive liar." Debbie said as she brushed passed him rubbing her breast up against him.

The Officer watched her back side as she walked away. He wouldn't mind getting up in that. Once she was out of his sight he turned his attention back to Jazz. "My name is Officer Thomas and I would like to ask you a couple questions about your boyfriend Dominick Taylor."

"Ex-boyfriend. I broke it off with him last night." Jazz revealed.

"Ok so you stated you didn't see him last night but your mother said you talked to him, can you tell me what you all talked about?" Officer Thomas pressed.

"Nothing much really. We was supposed to hang out but he brushed us off and we never met up with him. He told me he was busy and would call me later but he never did." Jazz uttered.

"How was he acting? Did he sound like his normal self?" Officer Thomas piped.

"He sounded fine. It was a lot of noise in the background but that was it. What's going on?" Jazz asked a question of her own.

"Mr. Taylor was found this morning badly beaten. He's in the hospital right now. We are just trying to account for his movement up until that time. Do you know of anybody that would want to hurt him? Or was he in any kind of trouble that you know about?" Officer Thomas babbled.

"No, no. He wasn't in any trouble and everybody liked him. This is crazy. I got to take the baby to see him. What hospital is he in?" Jazz rambled.

She was devastated to hear about Jarrett being in the hospital. Maybe this incident would show his how much he need to spend time with his baby. She picked up Jaloni and could see he was very cold to the touch.

"Something aint right." Jazz mumbled.

"Ma'am?" Officer Thomas asked.

"Something is wrong with my baby. He won't wake up." Jazz cried.

She begin shacking Jaloni but to no avail he didn't open his eyes.

"MA! Ma come here something is wrong with the baby." Jazz was frantic. "JALONI! JALONI wake up. Please open your eyes."

Officer Thomas stepped closer to the bed. Once he saw the blue coloring on the baby's face he knew the baby was gone. He reached out and grab Jazz to pull her away from the baby but she wouldn't let him go.

"No don't touch me. Get your mutha fucking hands off me." Jazz screamed.

"You betta watch your mouth in here!" Debbie rounded the corner with a scold on her face.

"Oh God please. Don't take my baby away from me. Baby please wake up." Jazz tried to pry Jaloni's eyes open but they wouldn't budge.

"What is you talking about?" Debbie asked as she stepped around Officer Thomas.

"Why? Why God? I tried to do my best to take good care on him. Please bring him back to me." Jazz begged.

Debbie stood back and watched as Jazz cradled her baby in her arms. Shock over took her body and she couldn't move her feet. She opened her mouth to say something but nothing would come out.

"Ma'am give me the baby." Officer Thomas tried to intervene.

"No! He going to wake up for me. He love his mommy. Don't you put your mutha fucking hands on him." Jazz hissed.

"I'm not going to tell you about your mouth again. I am your mother and will knock you into the middle of next week if you keep disrespecting me." Debbie uttered.

"Mother? Bitch you aint been much of a mother to me. Nothing I do is good enough for you. This is all your fault. I asked for your help. I begged you to take us to the hospital last night!" Jazz screamed.

The Officer had stepped out the room and radioed for the rescue to come assist him. He heard a lot of yelling and hurried back in the room. His eyes widen when he saw the mother and daughter up in each other's faces.

"I told you from jump that wasn't my damn baby and I wasn't going to take care of it." Debbie hollered in her face.

"I only wanted a lil help. I didn't know what I was doing. Why you wouldn't help me? My baby is dead. Look at him! Look at your only grandson." Jazz spazz out.

She walked back over to the bed and picked up Jaloni. She laid in the bed beside him and begin to rock him. Her world was flipped upside down

# Chapter 7

It had been four days since the death of baby Jaloni. Kiyara had been by her friend's side the whole time. She couldn't believe he was gone. After the police took Jaloni to the hospital an autopsy was preform to find out the cause of death. In their findings the baby had died from complication of Meningitis. The found out baby Jaloni had to have had Meningitis for over a week. His brain and spinal fluid was covered in the virus.

Kiyara got the devastating called early Saturday morning. She had to catch a ride to the hospital. After the doctor talked to Jazz and Debbie about Jaloni they all piled up in Debbie's car and headed back to the house. As soon as they walked in the house Debbie went in on Jazz.

"You a stupid mutha fucker. How could you not know that damn baby was dead? Unfit ass. If you had kept your fucking legs closed like I told you to this would never happened." Debbie hollered.

"Ma I told you he needed to go to the hospital but you wouldn't take me. You was so stuck on trying to teach me a lesson that you didn't want to help me out with him." Jazz yelled back.

She was done holding her tongue. Mother or no mother it was time for Jazz to tell Debbie how she felt.

"Oh no this aint my fault. You wanted to be grown so you should have acted like it. It's your fault he is dead. Don't blame me cause you choose a sorry ass baby daddy." Debbie hissed.

"Shut up! Just shut up. I can't take it anymore. You so fucking judgmental it's ridiculous. No matter what I do it's just not good enough for you. I get B's in school but hell you bitch about it not being an A. I made one mistake by having sex one time and getting pregnant. Give me a fucking break." Jazz barked.

"C'mon Jazz don't talk to your momma like that. Just calm down. I know you are upset but this aint the best way to handle this." Kiyara tried to reason with her friend.

"No she needs to hear this. You and I both know how she treated me and my baby. If she would have gave me just a lil support he would be here right now. Yeah he was my baby but I didn't know what I was doing. It was her fucking job to teach me. Kee, I asked her for some help to take us to the hospital but she just wouldn't." Jazz cried her eyes out in the crease of her friend's neck.

"I know, I know but it's going to be ok. I promise you it will." Kiyara consoled her.

"No it's not he's gone and it's all her fault." Jazz whined.

"You ungrateful lil bitch. Just so you know it wasn't my responsibility to take care of your child." Debbie said.

"Whatever you bitter bitch you. You going to get yours. Mark my words. Karma is coming for you." Jazz lunged towards Debbie but was stopped by Kiyara.

"Nawl this aint going to happen. C'mon let go. I'm not going to let you hit your mother." Kiyara pulled Jazz towards the door.

"Nawl let her go. I will beat that lil bitch down right there were she stand." Debbie threatened.

Kiyara heard the toilet bringing her out of her thoughts. She walked to the bottom of the stairs and waited for Jazz to come out the bathroom.

"Damn it Kee you scared the hell out of me. Where the hell did you come from? I thought you was gone." Jazz said descending the stairs.

"I was in the kitchen. How you feeling today?" Kiyara asked her.

"A lil better. I feel so empty without him. Kee he was the best thing that happened to me." Jazz admitted.

"I know boo. Have you talked to your mom?" Kiyara changed the subject.

"Fuck that bitch. I hate her ass. I swear I want to kill that bitch." Jazz vented.

"Girl don't talk like that."

"That's how I feel though. I can't stand that bitch." Jazz disclosed. "Anyways have you talked to Duce?"

"I wish that stupid ass boy would call me. Now that's somebody that needs to die." Kiyara added.

"I will kill him for you if you help me kill my moms." Jazz uttered.

"You can't be serious." Kiyara looked at her friend strangely.

"I'm dead ass serious. I'm tired of people walking around here thinking they can keep hurting me and get away with it. You herd the doctors if my baby would have made it to the hospital he would have survived. He would be here right now if that bitch would have just got up off her sorry ass and took us to the hospital." Jazz blurted.

"Do you know what you saying? We can't just be going around killing people. Bitch we can go to jail if we get caught." Kiyara reasoned.

"The key words id 'if' and we won't if we move smart. I've been thinking about this and I'm going to do it with or without you. That hoe got to die." Jazz retorted.

"You are crazy. I can't with you right now. Your ass done fell and bumped your damn head." Kiyara laughed.

"Say what you want but what would you do if you go to the doctor and find out Duce cheating ass gave you something you can't get rid of like Herpes or Aides. Bet your ass won't be saying I'm crazy then." Jazz replied.

"Girl my mind won't even let me think that. He knows I will kill his ass without a second thought." Kiyara responded.

"See you would kill him cause he did you wrong so why is it so hard for you to believe I want to do the same thing?" Jazz asked.

"Girl you tripping. I'm just talking over here. Your ass needs to chill on the killing people talk. I'm starting to think you gone off the deep end." Kiyara got serious.

"We will see. Hopefully you don't have to pull the first murder. Aint you doctor's appointment tomorrow?" Jazz smiled.

"It ain't funny and yeah it is." Kiyara admitted.

She was hoping her friend wasn't right. The issue with Duce was still brewing. He had been calling and texting her nonstop. She even seen him sitting outside her house.

"Have fun with that. I'm finna get dressed and catch a ride to Manatee to see Dom. He probably wondering why I haven't been up there to see him." Jazz stated.

"Have you told him about the baby yet?" Kiyara sighed.

"Nope but I think it's time I tell him. The hospital keeps calling me asking what I'm going to do with Jaloni's body. You already know I don't have no money to bury him so I'm hoping Jarrett can give me some." Jazz remarked.

"Yeah right. With a baby daddy like that good luck with that one." Kiyara hollered before running up the stairs.

Jazz shook her head and walked into the downstairs bedroom. She knew it was a long shot with Jarrett but she still had to try. She really wanted to give her baby a proper burial and if he said no she only had one more person she could go to. Her Uncle Black but he never knew about the baby in the first place. That was one well-kept secret she didn't tell him about.

Jazz dressed quickly and was out the door with in fifteen minute. She ran to the bus stop with only five minute to spear before the bus was due to come. As she sat waiting for the bus she saw Debbie riding by her with a smile on her face. This pissed Jazz off the extreme. Debbie was riding around town like she didn't have a care in the world. It was as if she didn't realize she had just loss her first grandson only a couple days prior.

Jazz boarded the bus with killer thoughts in her head. She paid her fare and made her way to the back of the bus were she spotted some empty seats. She didn't want to be bothered. She pulled out her cell phone and played on Facebook until she heard the bus driver announce her stop up ahead.

Jazz walked towards the first door she saw and waited for the bus to come to a complete stop. Once the doors opened she rushed off the bus. She still had to walk another two blocks before she was at the hospital. On her walk she begin to think of many different ways she could kill Debbie. She thought of torturing her first. Then an evil thought came to mind of chopping her body up into little pieces and then dumping her into the Manatee River.

Jazz didn't know which one she would do but she knew for sure Debbie had to go. There was no way she was going to let Debbie get away with what she had done. The police didn't see any wrong in what Debbie had did but Jazz just couldn't find it into her heart for forgive her.

# Chapter 8

"Look man. I knew you was going to get yourself in trouble. Now look at you. Laid up in this hospital bed damn there broke in half." Trizzey whispered.

"You aint tell me shit. What I want to know is why the hell am I the only one up here?" Jarrett gasped in pain.

He had three broken ribs and a dislocated shoulder.

"Nigga you the head. You took the job to run that damn block so you had to pay when you didn't follow the rules. Its aint like they didn't beat my ass too. Nigga my le is still fucked up." Trizzey explained.

"Yeah whatever," Jarrett huffed.

"We been holding down the block for you while you up here. The money has been right and there aint been no more fuck ups." Trizzey ranted.

"I don't give ah fuck about them damn blocks. Sell work aint for me. I'm out man. I almost lost my life." Jarrett admitted.

"You must be aint had this conversation with Black cause that nigga rolled up on me yesterday telling me you better hurry up and get back out there." Trizzey announced.

"He did what? Fam for real fuck him. He can't make me sell shit if I don't want too." Jarrett piped.

"Yo nigga you down gotten all us into this shit and now you want to bail? I think not. You better get your shit together." Trizzey raised his voice a little louder then he wanted to.

"Aye I didn't twist y'all arms to join my team. I'm telling you I'm out." Jarrett repeated.

"You not getting it. If you stop all of us are dead. Black said he will make all of us pay if his money stops." Trizzey stated.

# The Secrets He Kept

He was about to say something else but stopped when he saw Jazz standing to the door. He wasn't sure how much of their conversation she had heard.

"Hey sis. Bout time you got up here. I came by the house looking for you but your momma went off on me." Trizzey said hugging her.

"Yeah I been kinda going through it these last couple days. She mad at me and I'm not talking to her. I've been staying at Kiyara's house." Jazz told him releasing him.

"Oh yeah. Kiyara's grandmother letting you stay there?" Trizzey retorted.

He was shocked to be hearing that. He looked over at Jarrett who had been quiet the whole time. The look on his face said he wasn't happy to see Jazz.

"She in the hospital too so she don't know." Jazz revealed.

"Oh ok. I'm going to take a walk to the cafeteria to grab this nigga something to snack on. I'll give y'all some time to talk. You want anything?" Trizzey questioned.

"Nawl brah I'm good." Jazz responded looking over at Dom.

She could tell he was pissed she showed up there but the way she was feeling she didn't care.

"Alright," Trizzey walked out the room.

"What the hell are you doing here?" Jarrett snapped as soon as the door closed.

"I had to come see you. I need to tell you something." Jazz walked closer to his bed.

"I think you said enough on my voicemail. We don't have shit to talk about." Jarrett roared.

"Look yeah I broke up with you. I can't take you not being there for me anymore. You don't love me. You just want to keep stringing me along." Jazz blurted.

# The Secrets He Kept

"If that's the case why are you here? You said all you had to say. Just bounce." Jarrett uttered.

"I came here for two reasons. One because our son is dead. He died four days ago." Jazz whispered.

She let her tears cascade down her cheeks. It pained her to talk about it.

"So what. I didn't want the damn baby anyways. Maybe he is in a better place." Jarrett hissed.

His pride wouldn't let him let down the walls he had built up. In the inside he was steaming. He knew the way he had been acting towards his son was wrong but he couldn't show Jazz his emotions now.

"How could you say that about our son?" Jazz cried out.

She was taken back from his comment.

"Don't act surprised. You already knew what it was. What you thought that baby was going to keep us together. Now that he gone I don't have to say another word to your hoe ass." Jarrett growled.

"Tell me how you really feel then. I knew it. I knew you didn't love him. It's cool though he is in a better place and I'm alright with that because I know I did everything in my powers to be a great other to him. Your sorry ass on the other hand thought I kept my baby to keep you. Pussy nigga please. I kept him to face my responsibility something your dumb ass may never know anything about." Jazz went off.

"He wasn't my responsibility. I told your ass from jump to abort it but nawl that aint what you wanted." Jarrett mimicked.

"You sound retarded as hell. It's all in our passed now all I want from you is to help me pay for his burial. He needs to be laid to rest." Jazz panted.

# The Secrets He Kept

"If I didn't give ah fuck while he was breathing what's makes you think I will give ah fuck now that he is dead." Jarrett taunted.

"So you saying you not going to help me?" Jazz asked calmly.

At that point she didn't have any more fight in her. She just couldn't argue with him another minute.

"What part of no don't you understand? The N or the O. Man get your life and leave me the hell alone." Jarrett dismissed her with a wave of the hand.

Jazz stood there boring holes through his head. She let her mind digest what he had just said to her. She gave him some time to change his answer. She looked him in the eyes and couldn't see one stich of remorse. After it registered that he really didn't give a fuck about her baby she walked out without another word. He had just landed his self on her hit list as well.

Jazz bumped into Trizzey on her way on the elevator. "Excuse me,"

"Its ok sis. What's wrong?" Trizzey quipped.

"I hate that nigga. I swear I regret the day I met his pussy ass." Jazz snapped out again.

The old Jazz was gone and this new Jazz was telling it like it was.

"Hold on sis. Let go outside so we can talk." Trizzey tried to shhh her.

"Hell nawl we don't have shit to talk about on my son's grave he going to get what is coming to him." Jazz declared.

"Huh? On your son? What you talking about. You talking in riddles." Trizzey was confused.

"I'm sure your boy is going to tell you about it when you get in there. I got to go. You be easy." Jazz continued out the hospital.

Trizzey watched Jazz dumbfounded. He didn't understand one thing she had said other than 'On her son he will get what's coming to him.' He watched her until she disappeared around the corner. He marched into Dom's room.

"Yo I just got finished talking to Jazz and she is beyond pissed. What the hell happened in here while I was gone?" Trizzey inquired.

Jarrett had his head turned facing the window. Without looking at Trizzey he cleared his throat before he spoke. "The bitch done killed my son. Fuck her."

"She did what? Man you got to be playing. Jaloni is gone?" Trizzey ranted in shock.

"Yeah man. She let him die and then had the nerve to ask me for some money to bury him. She tried me." Jarrett assured.

"Tell me you told that damn girl you was going to give her the money for your son." Trizzey said out loud.

His eyes widen as he waited for an answer.

"Hell nawl. What the fuck I look like. I'm not giving that hoe shit." Jarrett declared.

"C'mon man you can't be telling me the truth. Whether you want to accept it or not he was your son." Trizzey was livid.

"Fuck you and that bitch. I'm not giving her a dime." Jarrett finalized.

"You dead ass wrong for that. I'm out. I can't stand to look at you right now." Trizzey stormed out of the room.

He needed to put as much distance as he could between the two of them as fast as he could. The way he felt he could put a bullet in Jarrett his damn self. He had to go talk to Black to see if they could get an advance on their work. He didn't know what else to do. He had to find a way to help Jazz.

Jarrett let his tears fall from his eyes. He was ashamed of the man he was becoming. He never pictured his life to be that way. He was in too deep to turn back now.

# The Secrets He Kept

# The Secrets He Kept

CPSIA information can be obtained
at www.ICGtesting.com
Printed in the USA
LVOW01s1009120317
526915LV00008B/474/P